The water rose higher . . . and higher.

It was the sound of the water lapping nearby that awakened Kate. Still seated in the librarian's chair, she had fallen asleep. It took her several moments to realize where she was. The library was so still and silent, she could hear her own breath. The only other sound was the smacking of the encroaching water upon the wooden stairs, and it was that sound that caught her attention. It was too close. Much closer than it should have been.

If only she could see. She would have given anything for a candle, a flashlight, a lantern. Anything to break this thick black curtain and take away her feeling of helplessness. How could she do anything useful if she couldn't *see*?

It wasn't the darkness she was frightened of. It was the water, so stubborn, so persistent, climbing ever higher. Without a light, how could she tell how close it was getting?

Med Center

Virus

Flood

Fire

DIANE HOH

flood

SCHOLASTIC INC.
New York Toronto London Auckland Sydney

ISBN 0-590-54323-7

Text copyright © 1996 by Diane Hoh. All rights reserved. Published by Scholastic Inc.

12 11 10 9 8 7 6 5 4 3 2   6 7 8 9/9 0 1/0

Printed in the U.S.A.   01

First Scholastic printing, August 1996

MED CENTER

flood

prologue

It began raining in Grant, Massachusetts, at 11:23 on a Tuesday night in mid-September. It rained lightly at first — a pleasant, refreshing, early autumn shower. Gardeners all over the city welcomed it, after ten straight days with no moisture for their fall gardens and the last of their roses.

During that night and most of the next day, the parched ground eagerly soaked up the falling rain.

But by the following evening, as commuters were making their way home, the pleasant shower turned nasty, throwing a temper tantrum. The wind rose, tearing at limbs of the huge old trees lining both sides of Linden Hill Boulevard, the main artery between the east and west sides of town. The skies turned an ominous black and, seconds later, opened, dumping thick torrents of rain on the city, flooding streets with deep washes of water, and snarling traffic throughout the city. Already-saturated ground refused to accept this additional drink of water, and spit it back up, spilling it out into the streets. Stubborn drivers intent on making it home drove through rushing pockets of water at low-lying intersections, a mistake that resulted in wet, ineffective brakes, causing a series of "fender bender" accidents throughout the city.

The Revere River began to swell, edging up the riverbanks on both sides like water filling a bathtub.

On the west side of the river, nestled on a knoll in the heart of the city, the world-famous medical complex known as Med Center stood staunchly against the onslaught of rain and wind. At Grant Memorial Hospital, Astrid Thompson, head nurse in Emergency Services, peered out a rain-streaked window and exclaimed, "Oh, great! A storm during rush hour. Just what we need. *Step lively,* everyone, it's going to be an interesting night!"

It was.

chapter
1

The medical complex known as Med Center, eighteen red brick buildings of varying shapes and sizes, sat up on a knoll in the very heart of the city — a jewel in the center of a crown. On the lush, meticulously landscaped grounds, seventeen of the buildings encircled the tallest and busiest of the hospitals, Grant Memorial, creating a giant wheel whose spokes were the glass-enclosed passageways leading from one building to another.

There was not a medical need that couldn't be addressed at Med Center. People from all over the world came to the Oncology building for its state-of-the-art cancer treatments. They came to the Llewelyn T. Grant Psychiatric Hospital, to the Hannah Rose Grant Women's and Children's Hospital, to the Dorcas Peterson Rehabilitation Center to seek treatment, cures, and advice. They came to all of the hospitals in the facility because they wanted, needed, the best. And the best was what they got. Because only the best were allowed the privilege of working at world-famous Med Center in Grant, Massachusetts.

Aside from the expertise offered there, it was a beautiful place. Lush woods bordered the vast acreage, and beyond the woods the Revere River ambled peacefully through the city, sparkling on sunny days like freshly polished silver.

Some days, however, were not sunny. There was no sun during the storm that hit the city on a Wednesday evening in September, when the charcoal skies opened and thick sheets of rain began falling on the complex and the shops, churches, schools, and residential areas surrounding it. The Revere River stopped sparkling and turned a muddy brown. It swelled rapidly and instead of ambling, it began to rush through the city as if late for an appointment.

"Hey, look, it's pouring! Now I won't be able to go dancing tonight. Life is just full of disappointments, right, Abby?"

Abby O'Connor, wearing a pink volunteer's smock over jeans and a pink turtleneck sweater, her dark, curly hair piled casually on top of her head, was standing at one of the big, wide picture windows in the Rehabilitation Hospital, looking out in dismay at the thick curtain of rain slapping against the glass. She jumped, startled, when the voice sounded at her elbow. Sid Costello had pulled up alongside her so quietly, she hadn't heard a sound. She whirled to face him. "Sid! Give me some warning, okay? That wheelchair isn't called Quiet-Ride for nothing. You'd make a great spy—no one would ever hear you coming."

"Oh, you bet. Must be all kinds of government agencies searching worldwide for an operative in a wheelchair." His voice was bitter. "I'll have to give that some thought. The best part would be, no one would ever notice me skulking around in doorways, listening at keyholes. You become invisible when you live in a wheelchair. People see a wheelchair and immediately look away. Perfect for a spy, if you ask me." He glanced up at Abby, his thick, dark eyebrows lifted skeptically. "Right? From now on, just think of me as Agent Costello. Have to have a code name, though. Something catchy." His eyes boring into hers, he said, "How does 'Useless' strike you?"

Her own eyes, round and dark and thickly lashed, held a mixture of compassion and exasperation as she returned his gaze. He was wrapped in a white terry cloth robe with his initials embroidered in navy blue on the chest pocket. The feet he had referred to as "useless" were encased in maroon hospital slippers. Whenever Abby saw those feet, her heart twisted in pain for Sid. Until a couple of months ago, he'd been one of Grant High School's star football players. And a great dancer. "You're not useless. You could even dance if you wanted to, Sid. I've been to some of the dances they hold right here in Rehab. Lots of people in chairs get out there on the floor. Sometimes by themselves, sometimes with a partner either pushing the chair or sitting on the patient's lap. They always look like they're having fun."

Sid turned his head toward the rain-streaked window, regarding with a morose stare the moisture shrouding the glass. "Right. And I'll bet it'd be even *more* fun at one of the dances at Grant High, where I'd be the *only* person in a wheelchair. Wouldn't *that* be a blast? Think of the attention I'd get. Probably be almost as good as scoring a touchdown, right?"

Abby stood her ground under his cold gaze. She was finally getting used to Sid's moods. "I wasn't talking about when you get out of here and go back to school. I was talking about *now!*"

"There isn't any *now!*" he said angrily. "That's what you people just don't get. All you do-gooding volunteers. You're as bad as my sadistic physical therapists with their master's degrees in Pain and Torture. None of you get it! 'Now' is about what someone is *doing*. People say 'I'm going to the store now' or 'I'm playing football now' or 'I'm dancing now.' If you can't *do* anything, there isn't any now. Get it?"

"Oh, that's ridiculous! People also say 'I'm reading now' and 'I'm eating now' and 'I'm writing a letter now!' You can do all of those things.

So you *do* have a now. If you were a quad, someone else would have to do those things for you." Abby was referring to a quadriplegic. Unlike Sid, who had been paralyzed from the waist down following a fall, quadriplegics were paralyzed from the neck down. "At least you can still use your arms."

Rumor had it that he'd been using those arms to spray-paint the water tower just before he fell. He and two other Grant football players had been signing their names on the white metal, there had been some horsing around, and Sid had gone over the side.

He answered her sarcastically. "You're absolutely right, O'Connor. What's wrong with me, anyway, being so ungrateful? I keep forgetting how really lucky I am. Good thing I have you to remind me, Little Miss Sunshine."

Abby's cheeks flamed. A couple of the older doctors called her that, but with a smile and in a completely different tone of voice. Sid meant it as an insult. He was saying that she didn't understand how he felt. That hurt.

She did understand. Maybe not completely, because she'd never been paralyzed. Hadn't ever been sick, really. But she had an imagination, didn't she? Did he really think she couldn't guess how awful it was for him? One minute he'd been a popular, gorgeous, dark-haired god of a football player, in fantastic physical condition. The girls at Grant High called him "Sid the Bod." Then, in one tiny, horrible little second, Sid Costello had tumbled over the side of the tall, old water tower. And this time, Sid hadn't rolled over and jumped to his feet, the way he always did when he'd been tackled on the football field. He wouldn't *ever* jump to his feet again. At least, it looked that way now.

He was still gorgeous. Nothing had happened to his face, or the thick, curly hair on his head. But his legs no longer worked.

She *did* understand. She could feel the shock, when he'd first awakened and found himself in an ambulance racing for Med Center. Then another shock when he awakened again later, in a hospital bed, with a tube down his throat to help him breathe, and no feeling in his lower body. She could feel the horror when he had realized that he couldn't move his legs, couldn't walk, couldn't run or jog or play football or dance. He must have been terrified.

No one seemed to know yet whether or not the condition was permanent. The wheelchair that Sid Costello was sitting in could be his for life.

Just thinking about it now brought tears to her eyes. She swiped at them quickly. He mustn't see them. Although Sid regularly indulged in self-pity, he detested sympathy from others.

His girlfriend, a pretty, popular girl who, in

Abby's opinion, had all the depth and compassion of a fingernail clipping, had dumped Sid the very second she found out his wheelchair wasn't just a convenient mode of transportation.

Abby felt bad about that. But what made her mad was, Sid wasn't even trying. The therapeutic regimen at Rehab, like everything else at Emsee (her best friend Susannah Grant's nickname for the complex), was the best. People with injuries similar to Sid's came from all over the world to take advantage of the rehabilitative expertise. But Sid wasn't interested. He seemed to have given up already.

It bothered her that she couldn't seem to reach him. It made her feel stupid and inadequate, and when she felt that way, she wasn't her normal, patient self. Their encounters regularly ended with the two of them snapping at each other. And she often went home now feeling drained and frustrated. After a really bad day with Sid, she sometimes wondered if she should quit her volunteer work.

She took him back to his room. The tray she had brought him earlier sat on his table, untouched. "Are you going to eat your dinner or not?"

"Not. Get it out of here."

He wouldn't let her help him into bed, insisting instead on parking his wheelchair at the window. He was still staring out into the night when, her back stiff with anger and frustration, she left with the tray.

The blackening sky had turned the city of Grant as dark as night. The rain cut visibility down to zero, making driving extremely hazardous. The fender bender accident victims began arriving at Grant Memorial's ER on the grounds of Med Center shortly after four o'clock, as people began leaving school and work in large numbers.

Two patients quickly became four, then seven, then ten. After that, there was a steady stream of incoming traffic. Gurneys raced back and forth from ambulances to the hallway outside the trauma rooms, where critical patients were first seen, and to treatment rooms, where less serious injuries were dealt with. As soon as a patient had been removed to an examination table, that empty gurney was wheeled away again, ready for its next load.

Most of the injuries were minor. A broken wrist, shallow lacerations on foreheads and chins, a sprained ankle. A recent safety campaign had made Grant residents more aware of the benefits of seat belts, and most people were using them.

But not all. Kate Thompson, one of only two high school students who, as volunteers, had been given access to the treatment rooms in Emergency, glanced down at the woman lying on the wheeled stretcher. Her nose was obviously broken, and both eyes were already beginning to blacken. There was a deep laceration on her chin, another slashed across her forehead. Kate had seen many accident victims since she'd begun volunteering and she guessed correctly that this woman, whose car had slid on the slick road and skidded into a utility pole, had been picked up by the force of the collision and tossed across the front seat, her head slamming into the passenger's window. Her carelessness in ignoring the seat belt had nearly cost her her life.

I am not here to judge, Kate told herself sternly. I am *not* here to judge. I'm here to help. She held the woman's medical chart, just begun, in her hands and stood off to one side recording vital statistics as the doctors and nurses checked for chest trauma. When one of the doctors called for a portable X ray, it was Kate who ran to get it. Tall and lean, her dark skin contrasting with the pale pink of her smock, her hair neatly cornrowed, she moved swiftly and efficiently. She never argued with an order from medical personnel. Her mother, head nurse Astrid Thompson, had said more than once, "Med Center is the *only* place you don't question an order, Kate. I only wish you were that cooperative at home." But she usually smiled as she said it.

Kate didn't question orders from ER's staff because she knew it was a privilege for a high school student to be allowed into trauma and treatment rooms. She wasn't about to throw that away by pretending to know more than her training had taught her.

The process of applying for access to the treatment rooms had been a grueling one. So many questions, so many classes, so many tests. She had passed them all. So had Susannah Grant. Big surprise there. The last person Kate had expected to show up on that first day of volunteering was the daughter of the richest, most powerful man in town. Samuel Grant II practically owned the entire city. His ancestors had founded it, had established the world-famous medical center, the University, and Grant Pharmaceuticals, a mammoth research and development facility on the grounds of Med Center. Susannah Grant could have anything in the world that she wanted. It was hard to believe that what she wanted was to volunteer in ER.

But truth be told, she was good at it. Another surprise. And she was nice. Never once had Susannah been stupid enough to say to Kate, as some white girls had on occasion, "I just *love* the color of your skin. Me, I don't even tan well." Comments like that still made her sick. They were so condescending. If they liked the color of her skin so much, why was it they never invited her to their parties? Not that she'd go, of course.

When the woman had been sedated and a

doctor had begun sewing up the lacerations with neat, precise sutures, Kate left the treatment room, wondering which room Susannah was in. She hadn't seen her in a while. It had been so hectic the last hour or so, it was hard to keep track of the rest of the staff.

Will Jackson, a paramedic and a classmate of Kate's at Grant High, passed her then, with two of his fellow paramedics. Their navy blue wind-breakers dripped water on the white tile as they ran, rushing a gurney along the noisy hallway through a crowd of people waiting to be treated for minor sprains, and cuts and bumps on the head. As he went, Will rattled off vital statistics to the doctor and nurse who met them at the door.

"Auto wreck," Will told the team, his words rushing together without pause, "thirty-year-old male . . . no seat belt . . . blunt trauma to the chest . . . some chest pain . . . tenderness in abdomen, upper left quadrant." The gurney rounded a corner, aiming for treatment room four. "Pulse one thirty-six," one of Will's part-ners said. "Respiration thirty-six and labored, BP one-twenty over ninety."

Kate fingered one of the heavy wooden ear-rings she was wearing, which she had made her-self. She held the door open so the gurney could slide inside the small, white room. Other doctors arrived, and the team began working in earnest on the patient, the fourth to arrive in similar condition in the past hour. Susannah was already inside, performing the minor but helpful tasks the two were usually assigned, so Kate left.

Will followed. He joined her at the coffee machine in the cluttered staff lounge. The white tile floor was muddy with footprints. Open bags of cookies and chips dotted the counter, and half-empty Styrofoam coffee cups stretched across the white counter near the sink. Kate bit back a comment about "the laziness of some people!" because she knew how busy they'd been this afternoon. There had hardly been a free moment to grab a sip of hot coffee, let alone find the time to dispose of the cup properly.

With every staff member working in one treatment room or another, Kate and Will had the room to themselves. "I've only been here for an hour," she said, "but in that time we've had more car wreck injuries than we usually get in an entire weekend. And rush hour isn't even over yet. It's only five-twenty." She poured herself a cup of coffee, adding sugar and creamer, keeping her senses alert for another ambulance wail. "You're drenched, Will. You look like you took a shower with your clothes on."

Will, taller than Kate by a head, poured his own coffee. He leaned against the counter, absentmindedly stirring the steaming brown liquid with a white plastic spoon. "It's nasty out there.

Coming down in buckets. River's already rising. We were skidding all over the road. Rush hour's going to be a nightmare." He handed her his coffee cup to hold while he slipped out of his sodden jacket and draped it over a chair. "I might pull a double shift tonight. If the rain doesn't let up, this place is going to be jumping. And some people won't be able to get here for their shift. How long are you going to hang around? Eastridge floods first. You should go home while you still can."

Both Will and Kate lived on the east side of town, north of the curve where the Revere took a sharp turn and headed south. "I'm not going home," she answered. "But I am leaving. I hate to when we're so busy, but I've got to hang out at the library tonight. Heavy-duty research on a science paper." Kate's sharply angled face softened with a smile. "Susannah's still here, Will, in case you didn't see her. Maybe she needs a ride home."

Before he could answer, a tall, very pretty girl, with shoulder-length pale hair brushed away from her face and fastened behind her ears, emerged from one of the rooms and walked gracefully toward them. Her eyes on Will, she smiled as she approached. "Talking about me? My ears are burning. I didn't know you were here, Will. I thought you'd left." Dressed in jeans and a white silk shirt, sleeves rolled to the elbow, she moved to the counter, where she pulled a tea bag from a canister and dropped it into a cup before adding hot water. The tea in hand, she turned to Kate and Will. Her face was oval, her skin peach-toned and smooth, her eyes a brilliant blue. "Will, you look like a drowned rat. Is it that bad out there?"

"Worse." As Will went on to describe for Susannah the deplorable weather conditions, Kate sipped her coffee, watching them silently. They made a striking pair. Will with his dark skin, hair, and eyes, Susannah Grant so blonde, her hair almost white. Two of the best-looking people in Grant, Kate decided. Susannah's twin, Samuel Grant III, known to one and all as Sam, was technically better-looking than Will, who had one slightly crooked eyetooth. Sam Grant didn't have a crooked anything. His face was perfect. But Kate liked Will better, so her vote went to him. And it wasn't just because they were both African-American. Will was smart, funny, and kind. She trusted him. Everyone did.

While Susannah's eyes clearly reflected her feelings as they settled on Will's face, his were veiled. It drove Kate nuts that he was so dead-set on keeping the girl at a distance just because she was a Grant and he was plain old Will Jackson from the east side of town where, Will liked to joke, "No white man has ever gone before. Except the tax collector." Then he would add harshly, "At least, no white person named *Grant*."

Maybe not. But there was always a first time. And Susannah didn't act like the rich white girl that she was, anyway. What also annoyed Kate was the way the rest of the staff kept Susannah at a distance, just like Will. They were nervous about a Grant hanging around. Afraid if they screwed up, she'd run home to tell Daddy. Which, of course, Susannah would never do.

"I was just wondering," Kate said slyly when Will had finished his weather report, "if you needed a ride home, Susannah. It's such a nasty night to be driving." She smiled innocently at Will, who was glaring at her. "I'm sure Will here would be happy to give you a lift."

But Susannah had seen the look on his face. Her cheeks deepened in color as she said hastily, "Oh, I wasn't planning on leaving. Not now, when things are so hectic. Anyway, I have my Be . . . car."

Kate knew she'd started to say "Benz," and then must have decided it would sound like she was showing off. It wouldn't have. Everyone in town knew Samuel Grant II had bought his daughter a gorgeous silver Mercedes-Benz convertible for her sixteenth birthday. Few people, however, knew that Susannah didn't like it. Kate and Abby O'Connor were aware that Susannah preferred the Jeep her father had purchased for the Grants' gardener, Paolo. She borrowed it every chance she got. It had more room, and Susannah said it was "more fun."

"When we do leave," Susannah asked Will, "do you think we'll have any trouble getting home?"

Will resisted the urge to point out to Susannah that he couldn't possibly answer that question, since they wouldn't be going in the same direction. Susannah would be going back to the west side of Grant, where she lived at the very top of Linden Hill, in a mansion that actually had a name — Linden Hall — while Will would be heading east, to a small white house that suited him fine but wasn't much larger than Linden Hall's six-car garage. Not the same thing at all.

Before Will could throttle Kate for offering his services as a chauffeur to Susannah Grant, Susannah's twin burst in through the door, his handsome face and blonde hair wet with rain. Spotting the trio gathered around the coffee machine, he called out, "Hey, who's up for a flood party?"

chapter
2

Kate, Will, and Susannah all stared at Sam. Susannah was the first to speak. "A party? In this weather? Sam, that's crazy. The river's already rising. Will said so."

Sam laughed. He reached over and took Susannah's cup from her, taking a sip and then making a face when he realized the cup held tea, not coffee. "Ugh! How can you drink that stuff?" While he helped himself to coffee, he said, "It wouldn't be a flood party if there wasn't a flood, would it? And if there's going to be one, what better place to view the festivities from than the fishing cabin?"

Susannah's jaw dropped. "The fishing cabin? Sam, you're not going down there, are you? That's on the South Side. It's right on the riverbank!"

"The cabin sits up high, Susannah. If the river rises, we can fish right off the verandas." He laughed again. "Quit worrying. Jeez, if everyone was like you, it wouldn't be much of a party. Fortunately, everyone isn't. A whole bunch of people said they'd come. Will, Kate, how about you two? Should be a blast."

He's only asking us, Will thought, because we're standing right here. Sam Grant gives more parties than anyone else in town. He has never invited a Thompson or a Jackson before. "No, thanks. I'm hanging out here. Going to be a pretty hairy night." He regarded Sam coolly. "You're really headed for the South Side? Ever heard the expression 'inviting trouble'?"

"Man, you guys really are a bunch of deadheads," Sam declared, finishing his coffee in one hearty swallow and crumpling the Styrofoam cup.

Kate noticed he didn't toss it into a nearby trash can. He simply dropped it onto the counter. Of course. Servants probably followed him around at Linden Hall for the sole purpose of picking up after him. "There's a trash can right there by your left elbow," she said tartly. "And since you're going south, how about dropping me off at the library on your way?"

"You're picking the dull old library over a Sam Grant party?" Sam asked, placing a hand over his heart as if he were mortally wounded, simultaneously gifting Kate with a grin. Susannah recognized it as the grin that melted young female hearts all across the city. She almost laughed aloud. A wasted effort. Kate wouldn't fall for that grin in a million years. She was too smart.

"Yes, I *am* picking the dull old library over your party," Kate said briskly. "Now, are you going to give me a ride, or do I have to hike through the wind and rain and dark of night?"

Sam tossed the cup into the trash can and sighed heavily. "I guess I'm going to give you a ride. Never let it be said that Samuel Grant III wasn't willing to rescue a maiden in need. Come on." Waving carelessly at Susannah and Will, he grabbed Kate's hand and strode away, taking her with him. She barely managed to grab her sweatshirt as she passed the pegs on the alcove wall.

"What am I supposed to tell Mother when she asks where you are?" Susannah called after him. "I can't say you went to the cabin. She'll worry herself sick."

"Don't worry about it. I'll call her. I'll take care of it. Relax!"

Susannah didn't look relaxed as she watched them leave the building. Rain and wind invaded the lobby as the door opened. "He's crazy," she muttered, "absolutely crazy."

"He said the cabin is on high ground," Will said. "Is it?"

"Not *that* high."

Then an ambulance arrived with two more accident victims. A house code sounded over the PA system, and staff members began running past the open door of the lounge toward trauma room six.

This was no minor emergency, Susannah knew. Her nerves began to tingle as they always did when a life-threatening injury arrived at ER.

"Don't get addicted to it," Kate's mother, Astrid Thompson, had warned Susannah and Kate on their first day of volunteer work. "The excitement, I mean. Some people thrive on the adrenaline that flows every time the doors open and you don't know what kind of incoming you're getting. We're not here to get that kind of rush. We're here to help. Remember that."

So far, Susannah's "rush" had come *after* a patient had been treated and she knew the volunteers had done some good, not before. Still, she couldn't deny that her adrenaline did get itself in an uproar when the crisis was obviously serious, as this new one seemed to be.

Two policeman, black slickers on over their uniforms, were filling out forms at the reception desk. One of them saw Susannah and Will heading for the trauma room and shook his head. "You don't want to go in there," he said emphatically. "Car hit a puddle, skidded, slammed into a utility pole, and caught on fire. There were two people trapped inside. Both your age. I'd steer clear if I were you. Let the doctors and nurses handle it."

Susannah hesitated. She had seen only two burn patients since she'd begun volunteering. A woman who had fallen against a space heater, and a little boy who had pulled a pot of cocoa off the stove on top of himself. Those burns had been serious, but not life threatening. The policeman's tone of voice told her that was not the case this time.

"He's right," Will said. "You stay here. I'll check it out. Maybe they don't need you."

Susannah bristled, although she knew he meant well. But he was implying that he could take it and she couldn't. She was hypersensitive about that kind of attitude. So much of the staff seemed to think that because she was wealthy, she had to have a weak stomach. Ridiculous.

"Kate's gone," she reminded Will. "I'm the only volunteer float left. I'm going in." She matched his stride as they hurried to trauma room six.

The patient on the table, surrounded by eight doctors and nurses, was conscious and talking. She was also coughing, in spite of the oxygen mask on her face. But she was not screaming in agony, as Susannah had feared. It was impossible to recognize her, her face was so black with smoke. Her hair had been singed, and her clothes had been either burned from her body or ripped away by the staff. She was partially covered by a sterile sheet, but the burn damage was clearly visible on her arms, legs, and upper torso.

Susannah swallowed a gasp of horror. Whoever that was on the table, she was never going to be the same from this moment on.

"Pete?" the girl asked repeatedly, her voice hoarse. "Is Pete okay? Where is he?"

"Why isn't she screaming?" Susannah asked Will, her voice low.

He lowered his to a whisper. "Her burns are too severe. I can tell from here. When you're burned that seriously, nerve endings that would be sending pain messages to your brain have probably been destroyed. Anyway, she's still in shock. It'll hit her later, if she survives."

Susannah moved to the table to take the chart from a nurse. Glancing down at the name, she gasped. Toni Scott. The severely burned girl was a student at Grant High. Susannah had met her through Abby. Incredibly bright. President of the debating team at Grant, a team that had defeated Susannah's private day school team twice. Toni Scott?

"Don't look," a nurse advised, pulling gently on Susannah's elbow to move her away from the table. "No need. You'll just give yourself nightmares. Believe me, I'm doing you a favor. The girl's in a bad way. Of course, she *is* still alive, which is more than I can say for the boy driving the car." After a moment, she added, "Maybe he's better off. If this one lives, she's going to go through hell recovering."

Susannah swallowed hard. And she forced herself to look at the patient. She had to. What kind of doctor would she make if she couldn't stand to look at a burn victim?

Although it was hard to be sure, with all that black smoke dusting Toni's face, it looked to Susannah as though her facial skin was only singed. But her arms and upper torso and legs were bad. Very, *very* bad.

When the respiratory technician who had been summoned stepped into the room, he balked for a second at the sight of the patient. Then he got a grip and hurried to the table, where he set up suction and prepared instruments that would maintain an airway for the patient. Her lungs were probably in horrible shape.

Susannah helped a nurse soak gauze strips in a sterile saline solution. When an airway had been cleared and the patient had been sedated with morphine, her burned limbs and upper body were carefully wrapped with the sterile gauze strips. She was covered with blankets and prepared for a hasty move from Memorial through an enclosed passageway to the Walter E. Miller Burn Unit on the grounds.

When she had departed in the care of two nurses and an orderly, Susannah returned to Will. "Do you think she'll make it?" she asked quietly.

He shook his head. "Maybe. I heard one of

the doctors say she was fifty percent third degree. But she's young and healthy, so if she's willing to fight, she has a chance, I guess. Pete Dawes was with her. He didn't make it."

Susannah didn't know Pete Dawes. And never would, now. "I thought," she said slowly as they left the room, "that most of the injuries we would have tonight would be connected to the storm. People swept off the road in their cars by high water, some near drownings, maybe, if the river really got high. Minor injuries from fender benders, things like that. I never once thought of fire."

"This *was* storm-related. That cop said they skidded because of a puddle."

"I know. But I still never thought I'd see a burn patient tonight. Not one like that, anyway." Susannah shuddered. "Sometimes I wonder if I'm really cut out for this kind of work."

"Well, stop wondering." Will put a comforting arm around her shoulders and held her eyes with his. "Because you *are*. There wasn't a person in that room who wasn't affected by what they saw just now, and one of those doctors has been practicing medicine for over twenty-five years. Maybe the time to worry is when you're *not* affected by something like that. But"—he stood back and looked at her for a moment—"somehow, I don't think that's ever going to happen to you. You're not the tough-as-nails type."

26

"A few minutes ago, I wished I were," Susannah said ruefully. "But I guess you're right. I wouldn't really want to be like that. I don't like the doctors who are. Nothing seems to get to them. It's like they're wearing full-body shields that keep anything from touching them."

"Yeah, I know what you mean." Will smiled down at her. "We'll make a pact, okay? When we're doctors, if I see you taking up a shield, I'll call you on it, and you do the same for me. Promise?"

Susannah laughed. "Promise."

Will reached out to brush a few stray strands of blonde hair from Susannah's forehead. As he brought his hand back down, she captured it in one of hers and held it for a brief moment.

Then three ambulances arrived at the same time, and they were off and running again.

chapter
3

"Are you really going to celebrate this atrocious weather with a party?" Kate asked Sam as he steered his sleek, silver van along the dark, wet streets of Grant. Traffic had thinned, and shoppers had abandoned the streets for their warm, dry homes. "The South Side always floods faster than anywhere in town except Eastridge. You could get stranded down there, Sam."

He laughed. "Sounds like fun."

"I don't think so. People died in that last flood. I was only eleven, but I remember. There wasn't anything fun about it." But Kate knew Sam had made up his mind. According to his sister, trying to change it would be as futile a task as trying to empty out the Revere River with a teaspoon. He was going to party, and he was going to do it on the South Side, where the riverbanks were too low to hold back rapidly rising water.

Kate gave up, falling silent. Her eyes followed the windshield wipers racing back and forth in a vain attempt to defeat the rain.

"You should come with me," Sam said lightly. "You work too hard. The library's probably closed anyway on a night like this."

It was Kate's turn to laugh. "Oh, right, it's a great night for partying, but not for studying? And they say women are illogical! I'll be *safe* in the library, Sam. I can't say the same for you, down there on the South Side. Anyway, I've got to get this chem paper done. But thanks for the invite." Like you really meant it, she thought cynically.

She had been to Linden Hall only once, delivering a jacket Susannah had forgotten at ER. Sam had been there. He had barely acknowledged her existence, sending a nod her way as he tore out of the house for soccer practice. Now he suddenly wanted her to party with him and his west Grant friends? Right. And the moon was made of chocolate chip cookie dough.

"You realize you're battering my ego," he said. "Choosing chemistry over one of my parties. Don't tell anyone, okay? It's too humiliating."

Kate didn't reply. She really didn't want to go to the library. What she wanted to do was head for home, make sure her family was okay. But chemistry was proving to be more of a challenge than she had anticipated. One of the conditions of her admittance into ER's treatment rooms was to keep her grades way up there. She'd need the grades for medical school, too. Even if partying *had* been on her agenda, which it wasn't right now, she couldn't afford it.

"You're crazy, Sam," she said, softening the comment with a smile. Sam was okay. Maybe not as compassionate as his twin, but not a jerk, either. A little spoiled, but then, most of the kids from the Linden Hill area were spoiled. They all had everything money could buy, and then some. Sam was no exception. Fifty-dollar haircuts and two hundred-dollar sneakers were Sam's way of life. He took all of it — the mansion at the top of Linden Hill, the silver van, the haircuts and clothes and swimming pool and sauna and boats and computers — for granted, Kate knew that. And the possibility of not doing as he pleased when he pleased (if such a thought ever occurred to him, which she doubted) would probably send him into a catatonic state.

At the library, she added one final warning about keeping an eye on the river as she jumped from the van. Sam grinned, waved, and took off, his wheels spinning on the wet pavement.

Well, I tried, Kate told herself. Yanking the hood of her maroon sweatshirt up over her head, she ran up the puddled walkway and disappeared inside the low, white frame and red brick building.

At ER, during a momentary lull in activity, most of the staff had gathered in one of the lounges to check out the weather channel. Will,

Susannah, and Abby were in the group clustered beneath the television set suspended high on one wall. The map was heavily green, which indicated areas of rain, and advancing rapidly toward the city were large splotches of yellow and red, which meant very heavy rain, probably including thunderstorms.

Someone pushed a button on the remote. A local news commentator stared out over their heads. "Police and rescue personnel are urging all citizens to remain indoors unless absolutely necessary. Many low-lying areas of the city are already flooded, and there are reports that the river is rising rapidly in the east and south. With more rain on the way, sandbag crews have been dispatched to those areas. Police are asking for volunteers. Do not call 911 to offer your help. Those lines must be kept clear for emergency calls. If you wish to volunteer, please call the number you see on your screen."

Abby thought the blonde woman in the red suit gazing out over their heads looked anxious as she spoke, and wondered if she had family in east or south Grant.

No one in the group jotted down the number appearing on the screen. They had their hands full where they were. And as long as ambulances were screeching to a halt outside of Grant Memorial every three to five minutes, no one was going anywhere.

Susannah could see that Will was torn. He lived in Eastridge. His family was there. That area flooded quickly, she knew. Helping to construct barriers against the river had to be something he wanted to do. But he was needed here at ER, too.

"Lots of people will volunteer," she assured him as they left the lounge. "I remember six years ago, when we had that terrible flood, they kept showing Eastridge on television. Everyone in the area was helping on the sandbag line, even little kids. Other people were taking boats out to collect people who hadn't evacuated in time. Some people volunteered at the evacuee center over at the Psych building. Everyone was helping."

Will nodded, and his frown eased a little. Before he could respond, he was called to ambulance duty.

Susannah decided to stay at ER until she was sure she was no longer needed. Abby wanted to stay, too. She wanted to go back to Rehab to see how Sid was. She didn't like the way he'd been acting lately. Even moodier than usual. But she knew she was needed at home. Her mother had recently gone back to work part-time, writing ad copy for Grant Pharmaceuticals, and Wednesday was the one day a week she worked late. There were five younger O'Connors at home. Moira was twelve and smart enough, Abby told herself, to come in out of the rain. But Moira would have her hands full with ten-year-old Geneva and eight-year-old Carmel, plus Mattie, who was only four, and Emma, still affectionately known as Toothless, though at two years and two months old, she no longer was.

"And it's raining!" Abby finished explaining to Susannah, who hadn't asked for an explanation. "The kids can't even go outside and play. Moira will be tearing every last red hair out of her scalp. I'd better go, Sooz."

"You didn't drive. I picked you up after school, remember?" Although the two were best friends, Abby attended Grant High, where she was a cheerleader and treasurer of her class, while Susannah attended one of two private day schools in the city. Sam attended the other. "Can you take a University shuttle, or would you rather I drive you? I can drop you off and come right back here."

"Don't be silly." Abby slipped into a copper-colored rain cape and yanked its hood up over her curly hair. She hoisted a huge brown leather shoulder bag. "Why should both of us get soaked? I'll hop the University shuttle. It stops right outside for the nursing students, and it'll take me straight to my house. Call me later, okay?"

Susannah was about to suggest they call the University, adjacent to Med Center, to make sure the shuttle was running in spite of the weather, when one of the short, squat, blue buses pulled up at the curb outside, its lights glowing eerily through the veil of rain.

Abby raced to catch it. Another chill, damp gust of wind rushed into the room as she left.

Susannah hated to see her go. Will was on an ambulance run, and Kate had gone to the library and wouldn't be back tonight. Kate's mother had left at three when her shift was over. While most of the staff was cautiously civil around Samuel Grant's daughter, Will and Kate were friendly and helpful, and Nurse Thompson tried very hard to see that Susannah was included in some of the more serious cases. With all three of them absent, it would have been nice to have Abby around for moral support. Now she, too, was gone.

But Susannah's brief lapse into loneliness ended quickly as Will, along with a young intern Susannah knew only as "Jonesy," and three other paramedics arrived. Two other ambulances, each with a seriously injured patient, arrived right behind them.

"Car swept off Bunker Road near Eastridge," Will said as Susannah ran with them to a treatment room. "Family in it. Mother, father, little boy. We've got the mother. Chest injury. Father and kid right behind us."

Medical personnel had been alerted to more

incoming by radio and were waiting in trauma rooms five, seven, and eight.

Although Will's voice was, as always, outwardly calm, this run had left him shaken. The station wagon with the family in it had been pulled over a steep incline by the rushing water. When the ambulance arrived, the car lay on its side far below them in a pool of water at the edge of a deep ravine. Will and his partners had had to tie ropes to the back of their vehicles and toss them down the hill to use as guides down the treacherously slippery slope. Donning harnesses, they'd clipped them onto the ropes before beginning the hazardous trip downhill, taking with them a Stokes stretcher, a resuscitator, drug box, cervical collars, the radio, and monitors.

The rain continued to batter them. Their navy slickers kept their clothing dry, but what they really needed was better footgear. "Should have worn my football cleats," Will remarked halfway down the hill.

Over the annoying, smacking sound of the rain as it hit the ground, they heard moaning from the car as they approached. Someone inside was still alive. Hadn't been killed on impact, hadn't been crushed when the car rolled over on its side, hadn't drowned in the deep puddle of water.

The first thing they had to do when they reached the vehicle was make sure it was secure.

If it had been in danger of being swept into the ravine, more ropes would have been necessary to secure it, wasting precious moments. As soon as they were positive that the overturned station wagon would stay put, Will squeezed in through the open passenger's window.

The driver, still in her seat belt, was a woman in her early thirties, lying on her side, unconscious, behind the steering wheel, her head resting on the windowsill. The sill had kept her head out of the pool of water, saving her from drowning. When Will checked, he found the breathing sounds clear in her left lung, but diminished in the lower right. Her skin felt moist and cool. He called for the resuscitator, which his partner passed though the window, and Will put an oxygen mask on the woman.

The car shifted slightly. Will held his breath. They'd been so sure it was secure. Had they been wrong? Were they about to slide off the road into the ravine?

The slight movement stopped. Will exhaled.

When he glanced into the backseat, he found a man, conscious and complaining of pain in his left leg. Lying on top of him was a small boy, fully awake but so dazed, he didn't answer when Will spoke to him. He was holding one hand over his left eye, but there was no blood on his face. A good sign?

The woman was obviously the most critically

injured, and required immediate attention. While Will slipped a collar around her neck as a precaution, his partners had carefully jimmied open the back door, which was now on the top of the car, and climbed in to examine the boy and his father.

"Eye injury here," one said about the boy. The father murmured, "Lollipop. He had a lollipop in his hand when we hit. Maybe the stick went into his eye. Is he okay?"

Using his penlight, the paramedic checked the eye injury. "I don't see a laceration. But just to be on the safe side, I'm going to bandage both eyes," he told the worried father. "That way, his injured eye won't move sympathetically with his good one."

Although the child complained that his eye burned, he was quiet while his eyes were bandaged. He had no other injuries, which Will considered a miracle.

After a sterile dressing had been applied to the father's open leg fracture, Will's partners immobilized the leg with a ladder splint.

Their actions took no more than seven or eight minutes. They worked quickly, as careful as possible to avoid sudden, sharp movements that might dislodge the vehicle from its spot.

Will knew the real difficulty would come when it was time to transport the three patients back up the dangerously muddy slope. The ropes would help, but both the woman and the man were unable to walk, and the boy couldn't see.

A call went out over the radio for more help, but they all knew there was a good chance no other ambulances would be available.

The climb back up the hill proved to be the most difficult task Will had yet faced as a paramedic. It took them, with the help of two men who had stopped along the highway above them, and later the crews from two additional ambulances, twenty-five minutes to get all three patients onboard. By that time, the woman's condition had worsened, showing increased breathing difficulty. There wasn't much they could do for her, and Will hated that. She needed surgery, and she needed it quickly, but the driver didn't dare go too fast. The vehicle skidded three times on the slick roads. Each time, the little boy screamed in terror, clearly afraid that his terrible ordeal in the station wagon was about to be repeated.

Although they remained constantly in touch with the hospital during their trip, the radio line was cluttered with static due to the weather, and they had great difficulty interpreting the messages from Med Center.

It was a harrowing ride. Will had never been so glad to see the tall, brick buildings appearing out of the darkness.

The woman was sent immediately to surgery.

The father was treated in ER by an orthopedic surgeon who then ordered him to another operating room. The terrified child was handed over to a social worker who would stay with him to await the arrival of the ophthalmologist treating him for the eye injury.

When the three had been dispatched to proper care, Will walked on shaky legs to the staff lounge and sank gratefully into a chair.

chapter
4

In the basement cubicle at the library where Kate sat at a small table poring over chemistry textbooks for her report, she could hear the rain slapping against the building. The library, usually busy in the evening, was nearly deserted. Kate had seen only two people upstairs when she came in, and one of them was the librarian. He had asked as she passed the circulation desk, "Not flooding out there yet, is it?"

"Not over here," she answered, referring to the middle of town where the library was, "but it probably is in Eastridge, and on the South Side."

"They'll have to evacuate," he said knowingly. "If the river rises."

Kate went on down the stairs, knowing he was right, and wondering if her family would be at the house when she got there or if they would already have gone to the shelter at Med Center. She could remember very clearly the spring when she was eleven. The Revere had risen so quickly during a deluge that many Eastridge residents, including her family, had had to be taken out by boat. At the medical complex, the Psych building, located a safe distance from the riverbank, had been turned into a makeshift refuge for people threatened by high water. They'd had food and hot chocolate and coffee, they'd been warm and dry and safe, and there had been a lot of jokes about getting free psychiatric care while they were there. But on the whole, the experience had been terrifying. They'd had to leave their home in the middle of the night, when it was dark, climbing out of bedroom windows into a torrent of cold rain and blowing wind. And as they left their small yellow house, there was no way of knowing if it would still be there when they returned.

The worst part had been when the water had finally gone down and they'd been able to go back home. Her mother had cried when they walked into the house, and Astrid Thompson did not cry easily. Their furniture, their rugs, the curtains, even the kitchen appliances, had all been covered with a thick layer of smelly, oozing mud.

They had all helped with the cleanup, a truly disgusting job. It had been three weeks before they could sleep in their own house. The musty smell lingered for months.

There had been heavy rains since, and some minor flooding. Every year in the spring and fall, they had storms. But until now, they'd been lucky. Except for basements, where all Eastridge residents had learned not to store anything valuable, houses had remained untouched.

Kate could only hope their luck would hold out. She couldn't study for a chem test in a shelter. Too noisy. And she didn't want to see that look on her mother's face again when she had to step inside a flood-ravaged home.

Pushing her worry from her mind, she immersed herself thoroughly in her studying.

An hour later, the librarian called down the stairs, "Anyone there? I'm closing early so I won't have to swim home. I'll be locking up now."

Kate didn't answer. She wasn't finished with her research yet. And if the weather didn't improve, the library might not be open the next day. There was a side door at the end of the hallway. She'd used it many times after a study session. She'd go out that way. One more hour should do it.

The light in the hallway snapped off, and a few minutes later, Kate heard the front door upstairs slam shut. She had the whole building to herself. With so much quiet, maybe she could finish in less than an hour. She'd catch a shuttle in front of the building, be home in forty-five minutes, nice and dry and cozy. Maybe she'd make hot chocolate. It was that kind of night.

She got up, moved to the stacks, put one book

away and took out another. Then, legs curled up underneath her, she settled back in her chair, content with the peace and quiet, undisturbed by the continued smacking of the rain against the pavement outside.

At Med Center, on the fifth floor of Rehab, Sid Costello, his wheelchair still parked beside the window in his room, reached out to slide the glass open. Wind-driven rain slapped at him and tore at his hair. Uncaring, he reached out to grip the sill, pulling his chair closer to the window. His upper body was still an athlete's. It took little effort on his part to maneuver the chair close enough to the opening for him to thrust his head out and look down. "Five floors," he murmured while rain soaked through his terry-cloth robe, "that's pretty high up."

"Mr. Costello?" a voice behind him asked abruptly. "What do you think you're doing?"

Damn those rubber-soled shoes! The staff probably wore them just so they could sneak up on people. "Just checking out the storm," Sid said in the same calm, even tone of voice he'd used in the past to make people think he was totally in control of a situation. It always worked. He'd learned long ago that if you spoke with certainty, people thought you knew what you were doing. Of course, he knew differently, but he wasn't telling. "Pretty rough out there, right? Glad I'm in here." Liar. He would never, *never* be glad he was in here.

"Look at you!" Nurse Plummer bustled over to his side. She reached out and slammed the window shut, carefully locking it. "You're soaked! Now we're going to have to get you into dry clothing, and I've got a bandage to change in 506, and back rubs in eight and ten." She frowned down at him. "We really don't have time for this, Mr. Costello. Not on a night like this."

Sid almost said, "What do you mean, *we?* I have all the time in the world. For now, anyway." But he didn't. Remarks like that got him nothing but disapproving looks. Everyone, including Abby O'Connor, wanted, no, make that *demanded,* a positive, upbeat attitude from him. But then, they weren't in wheelchairs, were they? Anyway, Abby had enough positive attitude for ten people, why did she need his?

He didn't have any to give her.

The nurse had locked the window. There was no way he could reach that lock from a sitting position. Not that he'd planned to keep it open on a night like this. Still, the fresh air had felt good. Why did hospitals have to be so stuffy? And with all of the windows closed up tighter than a bank vault, there wasn't any way for the smells of disinfectant and rubbing alcohol, and overcooked meat loaf from the kitchen, to escape the building. The stale odors were prisoners, just like him.

Nurse Plummer glared down at him suspiciously. "Is that really what you were doing with the window open? Just checking out the storm? You weren't thinking of doing anything stupid, were you, Mr. Costello? Because if we thought for one minute that you were, we'd have to transfer you to Psych."

Talking the whole time, she helped him out of his wet robe and into bed. This was the part he hated the most. Feeling so helpless. It wasn't the pain. They gave him medicine for that. Besides, he'd had all kinds of football injuries. He wasn't any stranger to pain. No big deal. But having to have things done for him, God, how he hated that! He would *never* get used to that. Never.

The phrase "transfer you to Psych" jolted him. She thought he'd been thinking about jumping? That made him mad. He was no coward! She could ask anyone. They'd all say that Sid Costello was no coward.

"We know that depression is common in cases like yours." The nurse pulled the blanket up over his legs. "You've had a rotten break, and that's the truth. That's why we feel it's important that you see one of the psychiatrists regularly." When he was safely tucked in, she handed him a clean white towel, gesturing at him to dry his hair. Her tone of voice changed as she added, "It'll pass, you know. The depression."

If she tells me how lucky I am, Sid resolved as he unenthusiastically rubbed at his hair with the towel, I'm going to throw my water pitcher at her.

"Everyone here is rooting for you," the nurse said. "You were an athlete. You're strong and healthy. There is every reason to believe you'll walk again. Why don't you just wait and see before you decide your life is over? That's always a good way to handle things." She smiled. "No jumping to conclusions."

"Actually," Sid said in a deliberately friendly voice, "I'm not doing much jumping of any kind these days, Nurse Plummer."

The smile disappeared. Two bright spots of red appeared on her cheeks. She plopped the buzzer in his lap. "If you need anything, just buzz." Then she was gone.

He was alone again, with the window closed and locked. A feeling of isolation swept over Sid. He was used to having hordes of people around at games, at practices, at school, at parties and dances. Now, here he was all alone, shut up in this coffin of a room. So much white. Why couldn't they paint the walls green or red or orange?

When the storm ended, maybe he could complain about the room being stuffy, and talk some sweet, innocent, young nurse into opening the window for him.

Sid was suddenly very, very tired. He might as well give it up for tonight and get some sleep. It was only seven o'clock. But it wasn't like he had plans. He wasn't going anywhere.

He fell asleep chuckling bitterly to himself over the nurse's choice of words. "Jumping to conclusions." If he ever did what she was worried about, the conclusion he'd be jumping to would be his *own*. Dumb idea. Really dumb.

He had just wanted some fresh air, that was all.

O'Connor should have stayed, Sid thought angrily as he drifted off to the sound of rain pounding incessantly against the windows. If she'd been here, I wouldn't have opened the window, and the nurse wouldn't have written down on my chart what she's probably writing at this moment. That I need to be watched.

Abby shouldn't have left.

He fell asleep and, as he often did, dreamed of the accident that had sent him to Med Center in a shrieking ambulance on a hot, sticky night in July.

They were bored, he and Rick and Santos. Too broke for a movie, too broke even to rent one. But Sid had enough gas in his car to drive out to the water tower. Rick's idea. "We're going to be seniors," he said. "Seniors always sign the tower. Why wait until school starts? Why not do it right now, get a head start on the other guys?"

Sid and Santos didn't argue with him, mostly because they couldn't think of any better way to spend a summer night.

It was easy climbing up the ladder leading to the top of the fat, white water tower on the outskirts of town. A three-quarter moon lit the fields surrounding the tower, and Santos had brought a flashlight. They stood at the very top for a few minutes, laughing triumphantly, giddy with the headiness of being so high up.

They wrote their names. Rick's was, of course, larger than Sid's or Santos's.

Then (and Sid could never remember this part very well), Santos made a crack about Rick being an egomaniac, taking up practically half the tower with his name, leaving very little room for anyone else. Rick laughed and swept an arm sideways in a gesture that meant "Get outa here." Santos knocked the arm away, Rick swept it back again, and they began wrestling in earnest. Sid was leaning against the railing, facing the tower, studying his name in black paint and feeling satisfied with the way it looked against all that white, when Rick's linebacking arm slammed into the side of his chest, lifting Sid's feet off the ground and knocking him off-balance.

He knew he was going to fall. Knew it even before he toppled over the railing, knew it before he felt the loss of a solid surface beneath his feet, knew it before the rush of air around him made him dizzy. His head filled with blood as he spiraled downward; his arms flew out as if he could suddenly, magically, create wings and save himself from the cold, hard ground.

No wings sprouted.

The next thing Sid was aware of was the calm, reassuring voice of Will Jackson, a football teammate of his. There seemed to be a red, spinning light behind Will's head, and Will was telling Sid not to move.

No problem there. Sid had already tried, when he first regained consciousness and realized slowly that he was lying flat on his back on the ground, to get back on his feet. Had tried really hard. Felt stupid lying there on the ground with Santos and Rick, weird looks on their faces, staring down at him. But his efforts had failed. He had used all of the strength he had, expecting to rise without a problem, just as he did on the football field. He'd get up, dust himself off, and stay away from water towers from now on.

It hadn't happened. In his dazed state, it had taken him a while to realize what the problem was, but it had finally hit him. The problem was, he couldn't jump to his feet because he couldn't *feel* his feet, or his legs. They were still there, he could see them clearly. But . . . it didn't *feel* like they were still there.

That terrified him.

But Santos and Rick were staring down at him, and Will was asking him questions, and, just like on the football field, he had to pretend it didn't hurt and he wasn't scared.

Will and two other guys wearing paramedic jackets were talking to each other, saying things Sid didn't understand. But what he did understand, very clearly, was the urgency in their words. And Will was frowning, looking as worried as Sid felt.

They opened his shirt and attached round rubber things to his chest, then hooked him up to a small machine. Then, although he had said very loudly and clearly that he wasn't in any pain, couldn't feel a thing, they stuck a needle in his arm and started an IV. He knew that's what it was because his grandfather had had a whole bunch of them when he had pneumonia the year before.

"What's that for?" Sid asked. "It's not medication, is it? I told you, I'm not in any pain."

"This isn't for pain," Will said quietly. "This is to keep you stable. You might have internal injuries."

He might be bleeding inside? That was almost as scary as not being able to feel his legs.

The ride in the ambulance was more frightening than Sid had ever thought it would be, if he'd ever thought about it at all. It was cold, and the light was odd, not quite yellow, not quite white. Like the inside of a lemon, he thought as he lay very, very still, hoping he wasn't shaking. He couldn't tell. His whole body seemed out of kilter, as if his brain had decided to stop sending messages to the rest of him.

The hospital was even worse than the ambulance. Besides the weird lighting and the cold, white walls and the cold itself, there were all these strangers bending over him, asking him questions he couldn't answer, and poking and prodding at him. Sometimes the only way he knew someone had poked him with a needle was when they said so. A doctor or nurse said, "Did you feel that?" and that was how Sid knew they had jabbed him. He hadn't felt a thing.

They scared him. He knew they didn't mean to. But there was so much *intensity* in their faces as they worked over him. It was frightening. He was in no pain, and would have allowed himself the luxury of thinking that he was going to be fine if it hadn't been for the expressions on their faces, and the atmosphere in the cubicle. You could *feel* disaster in the air. *He* could feel it.

They hooked him up to so much equipment, he felt like Frankenstein's monster, and they kept hovering over him as if they were waiting for him to rise and jump from the table. He wasn't left alone for a single second during those first few hours, and not much more than that in the following hours. Days. Weeks.

The last scene in his nightmare was always the same: the moment when his parents walked into his hospital room and he saw the looks on their faces. His mother might as well have hung a sign around her neck that read, YOUR LIFE HAS CHANGED FOREVER.

And at that point, Sid always woke up, clammy with cold sweat.

As he did now, on this chilly, rainy night.

They had all tried to sugarcoat it, he remembered in the dark of his room. Everyone did. Even the orderly who put him in a wheelchair the first time had said heartily, "Looks like a good fit."

A good *fit*? He didn't *want* it to fit. Why would *anyone* want a wheelchair to be a good fit? If it fit, didn't that mean you belonged in it? That you might stay in it forever?

No! That couldn't happen. Not to him.

Everyone said Med Center was a great place. It was, it was. Chock-full of cheerful, helpful people. Experts in their fields. The most expensive equipment, the latest in medical breakthroughs.

So why wasn't he walking yet?

Sid glanced over at the closed, locked window. It still ran with silvery rivulets of water.

5

When Abby O'Connor arrived home, dripping water on the parquet floor in the entry hall of the one-story, sprawling ranch house, she called out, "Hey, where is everybody? Big sister's here!"

"Alert the media," her sister Moira called from the living room. "I'm in here. Don't ask me where anyone else is, because it's not my mission in life to keep track of everyone."

Slipping out of her rain cape and tossing it haphazardly onto the coatrack near the door, Abby went into the living room. Toothless was playing with Tinkertoys in the middle of the room. Moira, lanky and already, at twelve, a head taller than Abby, was stretched out on the couch, reading. Mattie, four years old and the only O'Connor male child, was engrossed in cartoons on television and didn't even glance up when Abby entered the room. Carmel and Geneva were not anywhere in sight.

"Well, I *am* going to ask you," Abby said, walking over to crouch down beside the toddler, who looked up and beamed a delighted smile at her older sister. "Where are the girls?"

A shrug. "How should I know?"

"Moira, you're supposed to be keeping an eye on them. You agreed. When Mom went back to work, she said you could have the computer you've been screaming for, *if* you did your part around here."

Moira never lifted her eyes off her book. "I put a roast in the oven. I even peeled carrots and potatoes. I hate peeling things. And I've been keeping an eye on Toothless and Mattie, while you were off playing doctor at Med Center. I've done my part. *More* than my part, if you ask me."

"Were the girls here when you got home?"

"Yeah. I think so."

Abby sighed. "You think so? You let them go out in this weather?"

"It's just raining. They won't melt."

Abby got to her feet. "I'd better start calling around. If Mom gets home and they're not here, she's going to be mad at someone, and I don't want it to be me."

No comment from the guilty party.

Abby called every one of Geneva's friends, and then every one of Carmel's. No one had seen them since they got off the school bus at four that afternoon. "They aren't *out* in this weather, are they, Abby?" one of the mothers asked, causing Abby's heart to flutter anxiously. "There are all kinds of warnings on television. They're saying flooding is inevitable. You'd better find those girls."

As she replaced the receiver again, Abby's hand shook. Flooding? Inevitable? Not that their neighborhood was in danger. West Grant never flooded. And the girls wouldn't go out of the area without permission . . . would they?

Geneva would. And she could have talked Carmel into going, too. Carmel loved going places with her older sister. Their dad called Carmel "Geneva's shadow."

Abby returned to the living room and stood in the doorway. "Moira!" she called sharply. Red curly hair turned in her direction. "Are you sure they didn't say where they were going? Mrs. Conte says it's going to flood. They wouldn't have gone down to watch the river rise, would they?"

"Well, if they did, they're dumber than I thought." Moira thought for a minute, then said emphatically, "Geneva would, though. She thinks natural disasters like floods and fires and hurricanes are exciting. And she was only four the last time. She doesn't remember that people died and houses and businesses were totally wrecked." Her eyes widened. "If they wanted to see the river rise, they'd head for the South Side," she added slowly, sitting up straighter on the sofa. Her book slid down into her lap. She didn't notice.

When Abby said nothing, Moira asked in a shaky voice, "Even Geneva wouldn't go all the way down to the riverbank, would she?"

Abby looked straight at her. "You know she would."

"We should call Mom." Moira's voice was subdued, heavy with guilt.

"No, we're not calling Mom. Not yet. She'll freak. I'm going to look for them. You stay here with Toothless and Mattie."

"You shouldn't go out there alone, Abby. It's dark out, and it's pouring. Call one of your boyfriends. Make them go with you."

"There's no time. Keep an eye on the roast, okay? When I do get back with Geneva and Carmel, I'll be hungry. I won't want to eat charred meat, you got that?"

"I've got it." Moira watched as Abby put her rain cape on again. "Aren't you taking an umbrella?"

"In this wind? Waste of time."

"Abby?"

"What?"

"What'll I tell Mom if she gets home before you get back?"

"That's your problem. You'll think of something. You'd better."

"Abby?"

"What?"

"Be careful, okay?"

"Right." Abby hesitated in the doorway. She had hoped to return to Med Center immediately after her mother got home. She was worried about Sid. She didn't like the way he was acting. The spirits of most of the patients at Rehab lifted after they'd been there awhile, learning to do more and more things they'd thought they could no longer do. But not Sid. He seemed to be sinking deeper into depression.

But this was family stuff, and that came first. Glancing over her shoulder, Abby warned Moira, "You're in charge here. Don't forget that, okay?" Then she yanked the door open and plunged out into the downpour.

The phones were ringing constantly in ER. Susannah had taken over the chore of answering them when ambulances began arriving so close together that every staff member was needed to keep up with the flow. She was thankful that they'd only had one critical case since the burn victim. An elderly man from Eastridge had become so agitated upon having to evacuate his house, he'd suffered a heart attack. They'd brought him into ER in full arrest, but Dr. Jonah Izbecki and the staff had started his heart again. His wife and two middle-aged sons were still in the waiting room, sipping coffee, not talking.

While the major emergencies were the most intense, involving a lot of anxious activity, it was actually the minor injuries that took up the most time. Treating "criticals" was hectic and harried, but it went quickly. Those patients were speedily given the emergency care needed to save their lives, and then dispatched to the specialty area they required, either at Memorial or at one of the other hospitals in the complex. They never stayed in ER long.

The less seriously injured were not so quickly dispatched. And they had had a slew of those injuries in the past few hours, many from auto collisions. Because the vehicles had been traveling slowly due to the bad weather, the gurneys that came in one right after the other arrived with no great sense of urgency. Still, the treatments required created a backlog. Deep lacerations required careful suturing. Strains and sprains meant X rays, which took time, then ice packs or heat, depending upon the injury, and wrapping in Ace bandages. Possible concussions meant more X rays and an examination by a neurologist who, on a night like this, might not be readily available.

By eight o'clock, all of the treatment rooms were occupied with patients needing one or more non-life-threatening but time-consuming medical measures, and the waiting room and hallway were crowded with their relatives, waiting to see how the patients were doing, waiting to give them a ride home. The coffeepot in the lounge had been emptied and refilled half a dozen times since late afternoon, faces on staff members were lined with fatigue, and rubber-soled shoes dragged along the white tile as doctors and nurses moved dutifully from one cubicle to another.

Susannah had been doing phone duty for several hours when she answered a call, anticipating a question about a missing relative, and heard instead a very young, quavering voice telling her, "I cut myself. There's an awful lot of blood. I don't know how to stop it."

Susannah jerked upright in her chair, her eyes widening. She hadn't been trained in telephone emergency. Most people called 911. Those operators *were* trained. "You cut yourself? Where is the cut?"

"On my arm. I was letting my dog in the house and he was so glad to come in out of the rain, he jumped up and knocked me into the sliding-glass door, and it broke. Into lots of pieces. One of them stabbed me in the arm. I got it out, but now I can't stop the bleeding."

The glass shouldn't have been removed from the wound. It might have acted as a plug, minimizing blood loss. But a young child wouldn't know that. "Where on your arm is the cut?" Susannah asked.

"Here! Where my watch was. It's broke now, though."

On his wrist? Had he cut an artery?

"There's glass everywhere, all over the place. My dad's going to be really mad. But I had to let Jericho in. My mom says he's not allowed in the house, but the backyard looks like a swimming pool, and I was scared Jericho would drown." The young voice began to tremble. "Why am I bleeding so much? It's getting all over the floor."

The voice sounded male, but it also sounded so young, it was hard to be sure. "What's your name? And how old are you?"

"My name is Gus. And I'm seven. But I'll be eight in October. October eleventh. That's my birthday." The voice was no longer as strong as it had been when Susannah first heard it. It sounded farther away. "We're going to Chuck E. Cheese for my birthday, my friends and me. Eight friends. Because I'll be eight, see?"

Glancing around frantically to try to catch the attention of someone more qualified to deal with the emergency, Susannah saw no one. They were all in treatment rooms, stitching and wrapping and X-raying. "Is anybody with you? Where are your parents?"

"They went to get my brother at karate practice. Nicholas. He's ten. He gets to wear this neat white robe for karate. I didn't want to go, 'cause it's yucky out, so my mom said I could stay home if I just played Nintendo and didn't let anybody into the house. She said they'd be right back."

Susannah had no idea what to do. However serious the wound was, someone should be applying pressure to stop the bleeding. Would he be able to do that if she gave him instructions? Out of the corner of her eye, she spotted a blur of white, and whirled in her chair to see an orderly coming from a treatment room. Waving frantically, she flagged him down. Keeping the telephone pressed against her ear and covering the mouthpiece with one hand, she hissed, "Get an ambulance! Child fell through a glass door. Bleeding. Home alone. Wait'll I get the address. Don't move!" To the boy, she said quickly, "Gus, do you know your street address? I want to send someone to help you." With her free hand, she grabbed a pencil and a piece of paper.

"Thirty-one sixty-two Dean Street," he said. "Our house is red, like a barn." His voice was very weak. Susannah thrust the piece of paper with the address scribbled on it at the orderly. He took it and ran.

"It's raining into the house," the little boy said. " 'Cause the door is broken. My mom's going to be mad. And Jericho got mud all over the floor. My mom just mopped it after dinner, and now there's mud and rain and lots of blood on it. I don't feel very good. The walls look like they're

61

spinning." His tone became frightened, plaintive. "Can you come and get me, please?"

Where were his parents? How could they go off and leave a little seven-year-old boy home alone? "Gus," Susannah said firmly, "I want you to do something for me. Are you in the kitchen?"

"Um-hum."

"Is there a towel anywhere around? A clean towel?"

"In the drawer. Over there." He was probably pointing. She hoped he wasn't doing so with the arm that was bleeding.

"I want you to get one of those clean towels and wrap it around your cut, okay? Nice and tight. And then I want you to push down, hard, on the towel with your good hand and keep it there until the ambulance arrives. Can you do that?"

"Am'blance?" That really scared him. "Can't you come and get me?"

"No, honey, I can't. The ambulance people are very nice. They want to help you. Will you go get the towel? Do it now, okay? But stay on the phone, don't hang up!" she added quickly.

"Okay." Susannah heard padding sounds, then the whisper of a drawer sliding open. How far from Med Center was Dean Street? She had no idea.

"I can't put the towel on," he said, sounding very tired, " 'less I put down the telephone."

62

Good point. "Okay, put the phone down, Gus. But keep it near you so you can hear my voice, okay?"

"I don't feel good. I got to sit down."

Susannah was shaking. He sounded disoriented. Going into shock? That could kill him. And if the glass had indeed sliced into an artery, he could bleed to death if help didn't arrive soon.

She was clutching the telephone so hard, her fingers ached. Her voice rose sharply. "Gus! Gus, you can sit down. Go ahead, put the phone on the floor and sit down. Just don't hang up, okay? Are you sitting?"

"Um-hum." His voice sounded even farther away.

She thought she heard footsteps behind her, but there was no time to stop to see if help had arrived. "Okay, do the towel thing now, okay? The ambulance will be there in a minute." She hoped, prayed that was true. "But first you need to wrap that towel around your wrist and press down really hard, okay?" Had a chunk of glass sliced into an artery? Was that why there was so much blood? "And keep your ear as close to the telephone as you can, okay?" When she glanced over her shoulder, she saw that a group had gathered around her. Dr. Izbecki, three nurses, and the orderly who had summoned the ambulance.

Susannah immediately handed the telephone to the physician. He shook his head no and said,

"You're doing fine. Don't stop now. The ambulance is almost there."

She couldn't believe he wasn't taking over. He was a *doctor*. Wouldn't he know better than she what to say to a terrified child? Why was he making her do this?

"He's used to *your* voice," a nurse named Deborah told Susannah. "We're right here if you need us, but keep talking to him."

Reluctant, but deciding Deborah was probably right, Susannah said into the receiver, "Gus? You still there?"

He didn't answer.

Susannah felt increased anxiety emanating from the group gathered around her chair. "Gus?" she asked again. "Gus, where are you?"

"I'm here," he said in almost a whisper. "And I'm holding on to the towel, like you said. But it hurts. My arm hurts."

At the sound of his voice, an audible sigh of relief swept through the group. "That's a good sign," Dr. Izbecki said quietly. "That it hurts. If the wound was really bad, he probably wouldn't be feeling anything. Keep talking. Let him know you're still with him."

Susannah began talking again. Later, she wouldn't remember what she had said to the child other than reminding him to keep holding the towel tightly against the wound. She didn't hear the wail of the ambulance arriving at the

Dean Street house. But when the little boy spoke again, it was to say, "Somebody's here. I heard a siren, and now they're knocking on the door."

"Is the door locked, Gus?"

"I just remembered I was supposed to lock it, only I forgot. My mom's going to be mad."

Maybe not, Susannah thought, tears of relief gathering in her eyes. Maybe Gus's mother would just be grateful that her son was still alive. "Can you go let the paramedics in, or are you too sick? They'll come in if the door's open."

"I can't get up. My head is dizzy."

A moment later, Susannah heard the wonderful sound of voices, and a second later, Will said into the phone, "Hey, it's okay, we're here. You can hang up."

"No, wait! Is he . . . is he all right? Is he still conscious?"

"He'll be fine. Looks like . . . looks like a bad laceration. No arterial involvement. He was lucky. The place is a mess. It's a miracle he wasn't sliced to ribbons." Will paused, then added, "Talked to Dr. Izbecki a few minutes ago on the radio. He told us what you were doing. Now you know how a 911 operator feels."

"Something I *never* want to be," Susannah said. Her entire body, from her toes to her scalp, felt soupy with relief. She was totally drained. "Are you bringing him right in?"

"Yep. See you then!"

Susannah hung up the phone to an enthusiastic round of applause. With a weak smile, she stood up on liquid knees and left the desk, motioning to one of the nurses to take her place. She headed straight for the lounge, where she sank down on a couch and put her head in her hands until her head cleared.

She was still sitting there, leaning back against the rough tweed, when Will came in, his hair and jacket soaked. He walked over, sat down beside her, and put an arm around her shoulders. In spite of how cold and wet he was, she could feel the warmth of his hand through her smock. It felt reassuring, and it steadied her.

"You done good, kid," he said lightly. "Everyone's talking about you."

"And Gus? He's okay?"

"He's fine. Didn't hit an artery. His parents arrived just as we were loading him up."

"He was afraid his mother would be mad at him."

Will smiled and shook his head. "Trust me, she wasn't mad. Not at him, anyway. Mad at herself, I guess, for leaving him home alone. She thought they'd only be gone a few minutes, but they hit high water and had to take a detour. Anyway," he added, hugging her, "the kid wants to see you. He's all stitched up and a little groggy from the shot they gave him, but he keeps saying, 'I want to talk to the phone girl.'" He laughed. "People will be calling you that for a while, you do realize that?"

"I don't care." Though she was reluctant to leave the safety of Will's arm, Susannah wanted to see Gus before he fell asleep from the medication. "That's better than calling me the daughter of the richest man in town, right?"

"Right." Will stood up, too. There was admiration in his dark eyes as he regarded her seriously. "You're made of pretty strong stuff, you know that?"

She winced at the surprise in his voice. But she focused on the fact that he seemed very sincere. He meant what he was saying. "Thanks. That means a lot, coming from you."

"Yeah? More than it would coming from, say, Callie Matthews?" He was joking. Callie was the daughter of Caleb Matthews, Med Center's administrator. She spent a lot of time at the hospital, hoping to see her father, and both Will and Susannah found her demanding, superior manner annoying.

Susannah laughed. "Oh, please. Callie wouldn't know strong stuff if it walked up and bit her. She cries if she breaks a fingernail."

As they left the lounge, Will warned, "You do know this is going to be the longest night of our lives, right? I mean, you're prepared for that? Just be grateful that we're in here, safe and dry, instead of out there."

"Right." Susannah's stomach knotted as she remembered where Sam was. "I just hope my brother is okay."

"If anyone can take care of himself, it's your brother, Sam." Then someone called Will's name, and saying he'd see her later, he loped off down the hall.

Sam *can* take care of himself, Susannah echoed silently.

Even in a flood? a voice in her head questioned skeptically. He isn't SuperSam, is he, this brother of yours? Seems to me it's not very bright to challenge nature when it's on a rampage. Nature almost always wins.

Silencing the voice in her head, Susannah swallowed hard and went in search of the little boy whose life she had saved.

chapter
6

~~~~√W√~√W~~√W√~

Not everyone who had eagerly accepted Sam Grant's invitation to his "flood party" showed up. When those who had were gathered in the enormous main room of the two-story log house settled on a slope overlooking the roaring river, several people complained that friends of theirs hadn't been allowed to attend because of the storm.

"Nick's mother actually said that you were crazy, Sam," a pretty girl in a denim jumpsuit said. "She said Nick would go out of the house tonight over her dead body." Laughing, the girl tossed her long, silky dark hair. "Nick was standing right behind her in the doorway when she said that, and I could see that he was seriously considering taking a contract out on her."

Everyone laughed. A short, stocky boy in cut-offs and a gray sweatshirt said, "My dad told me, 'Go ahead if you're stupid enough, but don't call me when you get stranded. I'm not going out on a night like this to rescue someone who's too dumb to come in out of the rain.' " The boy's voice rose indignantly. "Rescue me? Like I can't take care of myself!"

The dark-haired girl glanced around her at the exposed beams overhead, the huge fieldstone fireplace, the black leather furniture. "I thought you said this was a fishing cabin, Sam. You'd better look up the word *cabin* in the dictionary. This ain't it. This place is a *lodge*. You could entertain our entire class in this one room."

Sam shrugged. "We fish from the riverbank and when the water's high, we fish from the verandas. That makes it a fishing cabin, right?"

The girl, whose name was Becka, moved to an expensive stereo system against one wall and inserted a CD. "Personally," she said, turning back to Sam as a slow song began, "if we're going to be stranded in a flood, we couldn't ask for a nicer place. It's gorgeous, it's warm and cozy, there's plenty of food, and stuff to drink, and the music isn't half-bad, either. Dance with me, Sam."

As he took her in his arms and they began to move across the hardwood floor, she added, "And we're perfectly safe up here, right?"

"Right," Sam answered heartily.

But as they danced, he glanced over her shoulder toward a wall of windows and French doors overlooking the river. The floodlights, on tall poles marching down the grassy slope, were on. He had noticed as they arrived and he switched them on that the river was already up to the first of three terraces below the house. He hadn't seen it that high since the bad flood six years ago, and then he'd only seen it on television.

And the water was still rising.

Only then did Sam remember that when the city of Grant had finally dried out that time, his mother had redecorated the entire first floor of the fishing lodge. Had she done that because she'd felt like decorating something, as she often did? Or had she been forced to by flood damage? Could the river possibly have come all the way up the slope and on inside the house?

He should have asked. He should have asked one of his parents if the lodge had ever been flooded, before he invited people here tonight. Why hadn't he thought to do that?

Because then he'd have had to tell them about the party, and they'd have clamped down hard on that idea.

Sam paused as they reached a telephone resting on a small table. He reached out, picked it up, and was about to dial Linden Hall when he realized there was no dial tone.

The phone was dead.

The fender bender accidents began to diminish as many people retreated to their homes to seek refuge from the storm. But the flow of patients into ER remained steady. Stubborn residents of Grant who had ignored the warnings on television and radio and insisted on going out into the night were swept off flooded roads in their vehicles. Some got out. Some of those swam to safety, while others, after being battered by the rushing waters, had to be rescued by crews scouting the city for such emergencies. It was those patients who were brought in with blackening eyes, broken or fractured limbs, perhaps a concussion from an encounter with one of the larger boulders in the river or a floating tree limb.

Those who hadn't made it out of their cars were less battered, with fewer minor injuries. But some of them had come so close to drowning that they had to be transferred through the enclosed passageway to the Elizabeth Grant Ross Cardiopulmonary Hospital. And some were rescued too late.

One of those victims was a young boy who worked as a page at the public library. Susannah recognized him immediately, even though his struggle in a car caught up in torrential floodwaters had drained him of any sign of life.

His name was Curtis Brock, a quiet, unathletic boy who had just turned sixteen. Susannah knew this because he had been so ecstatic the day just weeks earlier when he had received his driver's license in the mail. She had stopped at a local bakery to pick up a German chocolate cake Abby's mother had ordered, and Curtis had been inside, buying doughnuts. He'd been waving the license around, beaming with pride. "Now my mom doesn't have to drive me anymore!" Curtis had cried with glee.

Everyone in the store, including Susannah, had smiled at his unrestrained joy over turning sixteen and owning a driver's license.

Now, he lay on the gurney pale and drained.

That driver's license killed him, she thought angrily. If he hadn't had it, he wouldn't have been out there tonight, and he would still be alive.

The rational part of her mind told her it was the flood that had killed him, not the license.

He hadn't drowned, news that shocked everyone in the trauma room. What had killed him, according to the attending physician, a tall, attractive woman named Dr. Lincoln, was terror. Curtis Brock, she told them, had had a heart problem since birth. Nothing life threatening, and as long as Curtis led a fairly stress-free lifestyle, surgery hadn't been required. But, locked inside the vehicle bobbing and tossing in raging floodwaters, he had become so frightened, so totally panic-stricken, that the strain on his heart had been too much. "It wasn't the water

73

that killed him," she announced, "it was terror, pure and simple."

"I think you're right," one of the nurses agreed. She picked up a hand, surveyed it, placed it back on the white sheet. "Look at his fingernails. Ripped to shreds. The knuckles are bloody. Looks like he put up quite a fight before panic got the best of him. Must have clawed at the windows, trying to get out." She was an older woman in her late fifties, with lines of fatigue etching her face. She shook her head. "New car, one of the rescue workers told me. Electronic windows. Not a way in hell this kid could have opened those windows once that car hit the water. But they said there was a pocket of air at the top, near the ceiling, that would have kept him alive until they got him out. If his heart hadn't stopped."

Susannah stayed in the room after the gurney had been taken away. She helped put away the crash cart, wishing the paddles had been needed, that with the application of electrical stimuli Curtis Brock would have returned to life, as two earlier near-drowning patients had done. But, though he had been rushed straight to Med Center the moment he was pulled out of that river, his heart had already been stopped for too long. Even if they had been able to revive him, it was almost certain that there would have been significant brain damage. He wouldn't have returned to life as the same Curtis Brock that she'd seen in the supermarket. That Curtis was already gone.

It seemed bitterly ironic to Susannah, as she tore off the disposable sheet on the table and replaced it with a fresh one, that Curtis had died of terror at being trapped inside a car, when the last time she had seen him, he'd been so excited about driving one.

When she had done everything she could do to bring order back to the trauma room, she left it, closing the door quietly behind her.

Callie Matthews hadn't intended to go out in such terrible weather. Her hair, which she'd had done that very afternoon because who knew it was going to rain so hard you'd need a canoe just to get downtown, would frizz if she went out. Might as well just stick her finger in an electrical outlet and be done with it.

But her mother, who suffered from chronic kidney disease, needed a prescription, and she needed it tonight. Besides, the truth was, Callie *wanted* to get out of the huge, quiet house on Linden Hill Boulevard. She was lost without her best friend, Tina Montgomery, who had died at Med Center when a deadly virus swept Grant. She hadn't yet found anyone to take Tina's place. No one would ever understand her as well as

Tina had. They'd been two of a kind. "Privileged, pampered, and pretty," Tina had joked, "that's us. What could be better? There *is no* other way to live."

Brushing her hair, Callie winced. It hurt to think about Tina. So mostly, she didn't. But sometimes, it was hard not to. Like on a foul, rainy night when she didn't have anything to do. She'd been invited to Sam Grant's flood party, but her mother had said absolutely not. "You are not going anywhere *near* the South Side in this weather, and that's final!"

Okay, so she'd just run to the drugstore before any flooding took over the city. If it ever did. Probably wouldn't flood at all. People got all excited about things like that because they were bored.

Maybe she'd buy a new fashion magazine to read. And new nail polish. At the hospital the other day, when Susannah had made that stupid remark about how she'd rather drive her gardener's Jeep than that beautiful little silver Benz her father had bought her, Callie, aghast, had cried, "That is too weird, Susannah! You want to ride in a car the hired help uses?" And Kate Thompson, who admittedly always looked as if she'd stepped straight off the cover of a fashion magazine herself, had said coolly, "Callie, someone who wears nail polish in that disgusting shade of putrid purple for the whole world to see has no business calling someone else weird."

Callie's hands had flown behind her back so fast, her fingers had almost fallen off.

If gorgeous Kate Thompson thought Callie's nail polish was weird, maybe it was.

Normally, Callie wouldn't even think of letting someone from Eastridge dictate what she should wear. But Kate always looked so perfect. How did she do that when she wasn't even rich? And that soft, pale pink she'd been wearing on *her* nails was nice.

Maybe I'll look for something like that at the drugstore, Callie thought as she donned a designer hooded raincoat in a vibrant shade of purple. Then, remembering Kate's comment about the purple nail polish, she discarded that coat and slipped instead into a bright red one with a matching wide-brimmed hat that tied under her chin, and a pair of red high-heeled boots to make her feel taller than her five feet.

The outfit was pretty, but impractical. She was already drenched by the time she had run from the house to her robin's-egg blue sports car, which, as usual, she had left out in the driveway to show it off instead of parking it in the garage. She turned on the engine and the wipers. What an awful night! There was sure to be flooding, after all. Especially in Eastridge and on the South

Side, and Sam Grant was absolutely insane to hold a party down there now. Anyone who'd gone was crazy, too.

So why did she wish, as she drove down a dangerously slick Linden Hill Boulevard, that she was there, on that riverbank, in Sam's fishing lodge, instead of taking a nice, safe trip to the drugstore?

At Med Center, motorists stranded in high water, rescued by Emergency crews or fire or police personnel, continued to arrive in a steady stream.

"You're still here?" Will asked a beleaguered Susannah, who was trying to balance a telephone on one shoulder while her other arm struggled to maintain a shaky hold on a handful of patient charts. She was trying valiantly to keep track of each patient upon arrival, jotting down a name given to her by one of the rescue crew, if they had it. Sometimes they didn't. People who had been dragged from the wildly rushing river had, for the most part, been stripped of their identity temporarily. No wallet, no purse, no ID anywhere on their person. If they were conscious and not in deep shock, they were able to give a name, and Susannah quickly jotted it down on a chart. The unconscious ones remained unidentified, unless someone on the crew knew them personally and could identify them.

In response to Will's query, Susannah rolled her eyes heavenward. She glanced pointedly toward the crowded waiting room, filled with patients awaiting treatment, and relatives awaiting word of patients currently being treated. "Yes, I am still here," she said. "And I've decided I'm not leaving. Unless it stops raining. Then maybe I'll think about it."

It did not stop raining.

—√◊∧◊√◊—

Jeremy Barlow, on his way to Med Center to meet his father for dinner, was glad his father had given him a Chevy Blazer instead of the low-slung black sports car he'd really wanted. The Blazer sat higher off the ground. Jeremy had had no idea the weather was this bad. He hadn't been watching television, and anytime a news program broke in on his radio, he had quickly switched the station or turned it off and put a CD on his stereo. News was depressing.

It was becoming very clear to him that this was one night when he shouldn't have switched the radio station so quickly. The announcer had probably told everyone to stay home. Not a bad idea.

Steering the Blazer away from a deep pool that glistened under the pale yellow streetlights, Jeremy thought about turning around on the deserted road and going back home.

But he and his father had so little time together. Eminent heart surgeons like Thomas Barlow didn't have a lot of evenings free. If he wasn't operating on a life-or-death case, he was attending a committee meeting or a Board meeting or a fund-raiser for Med Center, or traveling out of town to give speeches. Jeremy had learned to make plans with his father weeks in advance. Sometimes that worked. Sometimes it didn't. On this particular night, there hadn't been any phone calls from the hospital canceling the plans they'd made three weeks ago. So why spoil it by worrying about the weather?

He kept going. There was very little traffic on this stormy, windy night. But negotiating the low-lying areas rushing with water took some doing. Jeremy tried to concentrate, but instead he found himself thinking about his mother leaving the way she had. If she hadn't gone away, maybe his father would be home more often.

Ha! Who was he kidding? Had his father been home any more often before his wife packed up a couple of suitcases and her laptop computer and left the house for San Francisco to become a writer? Nosiree, he had *not!* Wasn't that part of the reason his mother had left in the first place?

He hadn't gone with her, although she'd asked, because he hadn't wanted to leave Grant. Besides, his mother was probably going to be poor, and Jeremy knew he wouldn't be good at that.

Because he wasn't concentrating, he neglected

to steer around the next pocket of deep water. When he hit it, thick sheets of water sprayed upward, coating the windshield and splashing against the windows. Jeremy sucked in his breath as for one scary second, the Blazer hydroplaned, its wheels completely off the ground. The sensation was eerie. It was as if he were taking off in an airplane.

But an airplane was *supposed* to take off. A car wasn't.

When the wheels once again hit solid ground, Jeremy exhaled with relief. He focused his mind after that on driving, and made it to the hospital without any more scares.

There was no answer when he knocked on the door of his father's office on the eighth floor of Grant Memorial. Still in surgery? Sighing, Jeremy took a seat on a padded leather bench and waited. And waited. And waited.

He was about to give up when his father, still wearing his surgical greens, his mask hanging around his neck, came striding down the hallway. A tall, impressive figure, he smiled a welcome when he spotted his son.

I wish I were that tall, Jeremy thought as he stood up. He looked like his mother, average height, blonde hair, decent bone structure, nice eyes, but no distinguishing features. If he were taller, like his father, that would have helped make him more interesting-looking. But he wasn't taller. Five ten, tops. His father was six two.

"Sorry, kid," his father said regretfully as he joined Jeremy, "but I've got to get back down there. We've got a real mess on our hands. I told this guy a hundred times to quit smoking and buy a treadmill, but he ignored my advice. Got stranded in high water. Panicked, and had a heart attack. Now he's in serious trouble. Triple bypass, and we've run into some bleeding problems. Dinner's going to have to wait for another night."

Jeremy wasn't surprised. He was used to it. At least his father hadn't forgotten, though that wouldn't have been a surprise, either. "No big deal," he said lightly, hiding his disappointment. "Pretty nasty out there, anyway. I'll probably just go home and watch television. It's okay, Dad."

But it wasn't.

He wasn't going home to watch the stupid boob tube. He'd go down to ER and see if Kate was on duty. Seeing Kate, even if he didn't talk to her, always brightened his mood, no matter how gloomy he was feeling. When he was feeling sorry for himself, no one snapped him out of it faster than Kate, with her caustic sense of humor.

His second disappointment of the evening came when he arrived down in ER and there was no sign of Kate. Will and Susannah told him she'd gone to the library.

"In this?" he asked, waving a hand toward the windows, sheeted with rain. "She didn't walk, did she?"

"Sam took her," Susannah said. "Dropped her off on the way to his flood party. I thought you'd be there."

"Flood party? Your brother is actually celebrating this lousy weather?"

"Yep. At our fishing lodge on the South Side of town."

"You're kidding!"

"No. I wish I were. I just thought you'd be there. You always go to Sam's parties."

"I was supposed to have dinner with my dad. He couldn't make it. I didn't know anything about any party, but I wouldn't have gone, anyway. Not down there, not tonight. Your brother's braver than I am."

"You mean crazier," Susannah said darkly. "And I'll bet he got a whole bunch of people to join him, too. If anything happens . . ."

"Nothing's going to happen," Will interjected, smiling at her. He didn't like seeing her so anxious. It was hard enough that they'd had such a hectic night in ER. She should have gone home hours ago. She looked tired. But she had refused to leave, saying there was too much to do and the staff needed all the help they could get. He had stayed, too, but that was a decision he'd made when the first high-water victims began arriving. It had nothing to do with Susannah. Almost nothing. "Your brother can take care of himself. And anyone who's with him."

"Maybe." She didn't sound convinced, but her face had brightened a little.

"If Sam dropped Kate off, she'll need a ride home, right?" Jeremy asked. His bare head was very wet. His hair, usually neatly parted and combed smooth, had begun waving around his ears and forehead.

Susannah thought it made him look more relaxed. Jeremy was very good-looking, but his face always looked so tense. Will called Jeremy "uptight." Will was right. "She might," Susannah said. "But the library probably closed early. She could already be on her way home."

"Well, it won't hurt to go see," Jeremy said. "If she's not there, fine. But if she is, maybe she'll be glad to have a ride. I'll give it a shot."

When he had gone, Will turned to Susannah, grinning. "Young love?"

"Not in a million years!" Susannah laughed. And even though she knew he wasn't referring to himself and Susannah, because all they'd ever shared was a dance or two and hours of work, Susannah felt her face growing warm.

She was relieved when one of the doctors called to her then, announcing that incoming was arriving and she'd be needed to chart vital statistics. Grateful for the interruption, she hurried away from Will.

Dr. Jonah Izbecki was on call. He was a man Susannah liked and respected. He'd been wary of her at first, just like all the others, but after a while, he'd thawed. Now, he was one of the doctors who tended to give her more responsibility. This time, the moment she hurried into the treatment room, he directed her to one of the supply cabinets, asking for a second bottle of sterile saline solution to irrigate a nasty wound he was suturing. "Floodwaters swept this guy's car into the plate glass window of a store," he was informing the nurse who stood beside him. As if to fortify his argument, Izbecki held a large chunk of glass up to the surgical lamp. "Quit raining yet?" he asked Susannah.

She handed the nurse the bottle and waited for further instructions. "No. Doesn't look like it's going to, either."

Dr. Izbecki groaned audibly. He poised the long surgical tweezers over the chest of the patient. "That means this endless parade of unfortunates is going to continue. I need six more hands. Half the night shift hasn't arrived. Can't get here, or so they say. Why didn't I go into law the way my parents wanted? My eyes are killing me. Some of these glass shards are tiny. Pull that lamp closer."

Susannah reached out to obey. She was so tired, her body yearned for a nap, even a short one. But Izbecki was right. Until the rain stopped, the flow of patients would continue. Eventually, everyone would get the message, and the fender benders would end. People would stop risking death by drowning, and take to the indoors. Most of them, anyway.

But sooner or later, the evacuations would begin. That could mean people falling from ladders and roofs and out of boats as they tried to escape floodwaters. There might be fires as gas lines were split in two by the force of rushing water. People trying to leave their area on foot or in vehicles could be swept up in the flood before rescue crews arrived.

It's going to be a really long night, Susannah thought as she went back to the cabinet for gauze pads and adhesive tape.

Jeremy, on his way to the library, wondered if he was making a mistake. Should he really offer to drive Kate home? She lived in Eastridge. Wouldn't that be flooded by now? It always flooded first, even before the South Side. Did he really want to risk driving into that, even for Kate?

Maybe . . . maybe he wouldn't take her home. He could take her to his house. The west side of town never flooded. She'd be safe there. The housekeeper, Mrs. Lamme, was staying the night. He'd tell Kate that, so she'd know right away that he was just talking friendship, not romance. He wanted her to have a safe, dry place to stay, that was all.

That's not *quite* all, a nasty little voice in the back of his head told him. Be honest, Jeremy. Aren't you picturing the look on your father's face if he came down to breakfast tomorrow morning to find a pretty, African-American girl in his kitchen? *That* would certainly get his attention, wouldn't it, Jeremy? Isn't that what you're thinking about?

"No," he said aloud. "I'm thinking about Kate." Then he added reluctantly, "Mostly." And he continued steering the Blazer through the dark, wet streets toward the library.

Will came out of treatment room five, looking for Susannah. Her face had looked strained and tired the last time he'd seen her. Maybe he could talk her into going home. She could come back in the morning. She'd be needed then, too. If she stayed at the hospital all night, she'd be no good tomorrow.

"You have to go home," he said firmly when she came out into the corridor behind the gurney that was being wheeled up to X Ray by an orderly. "Things are going to be just as busy tomorrow. School will be canceled, so you can work all day if you want. But you need some sleep first."

She glared up at him. "Look who's talking. You've been here longer than I have. Are *you* going home?"

"Yeah, sure," he lied. "Not right now, though. Got a few things I have to do first. And listen, don't take that Benz of yours, okay? Leave it in the parking garage and grab a shuttle. Safer that way."

Glancing up at the big round clock over the nurses' desk, Susannah said, "They're not running. It's too late. But," she added with phony innocence, "since you're leaving any second now, I'll just wait for you and you can drive me home." She knew he had no intention of leaving. She just wanted to see if he'd admit it.

"Oh. Sure. I mean . . . uh, yeah, I can take you home. Why don't we go right now? I guess that other stuff can wait."

Susannah laughed. "Who are you kidding? You'll take me home and then you'll turn right around and come back here. Forget it, Will. I'm staying if you are, and that's that. Live with it."

He fixed his dark eyes on hers. "Man, you're stubborn!"

Susannah was so tired, she had to fight the impulse to lean against him, nestle her head against his shoulder, and close her eyes. She wondered what he would do if she did that, right out here in the hallway with a waiting room full of Grant residents watching. Maybe he'd faint. She'd have to haul him up onto a gurney and wheel him into a treatment room.

The image struck her funny, and she began laughing. Before it could turn into hysterics, she stopped, took a deep breath, and let it out. Then she grinned up at him and said jokingly, "I *beg* your pardon. *I,* sir, am Susannah Grant, a spoiled rich girl from the *very* best part of town. I live in a mansion fully equipped with servants. I do not take orders from mere paramedics. I shall return to the mansion when *I* decide it is time, and not one tiny little moment before."

He laughed and raised his hands in a gesture of defeat. "Okay, okay, I get it! I was just trying to be a little considerate, that's all."

Susannah's grin widened. If she hadn't been so tired, she would have let the remark go without commenting. But her brain was on overdrive and she wasn't herself. "Gee," she said lightly, "I didn't know you cared!"

And although an ambulance wail at the back door drowned out his reply, she could have sworn that what he said then was, "Well, I do."

Before she could mull that over, he was off and running again and one of the nurses was calling to her to bring a bunch of clean towels to trauma room two.

Thinking about what Will's comment meant would have to wait. Like everything else on this wild, stormy night.

Still, Susannah's step was considerably lighter as she hurried to the linen closet.

chapter

8

—∿∿₩∿∿—

Abby hesitated at the corner of Fourth Street and Liberty. It was raining so hard, staring ahead of her was like looking through a pair of dirty eyeglasses. But she could see that the side street she was on was deserted. The post office, the parking garages, the little boutiques, all were closed. There was no traffic, and deep, rushing streams ran alongside both curbs. She was still four blocks away from Massachusetts Avenue, the main drag that paralleled the Revere. If the water was this deep here, what would it be like there, where the river had almost certainly overflowed its banks?

And *where* were her sisters?

Head down, Abby forged ahead, battling ferocious gusts of wind until she reached the avenue. The lights were on at the drugstore to her left. She could try there. Maybe someone inside had seen Geneva and Carmel.

The upper half of the wide avenue, where she was standing, hadn't flooded yet. The banks up here were steeper. But farther down the street where the banks were lower, just beyond the arching stone bridge that crossed the river, she could see that the avenue had become a lake. The shops there were closed, but their interior lights, left on for safety's sake, shone out upon a swirling, muddy mess inching ever closer to their doors.

Abby's heart lurched with fear. She had to find her sisters. She whirled and ran up the street to the drugstore. "Please," she murmured as she ran, "please let it be open."

It was. Abby flung herself against the door and pushed, spilling out into a store empty but for three people. The owners, an elderly couple, stood behind the prescription counter talking to a small, thin girl in a bright red raincoat, matching hat, and high-heeled red boots. She turned around when the door burst open.

Abby recognized the girl and groaned silently. Callie Matthews. If she was going to run into anyone, why did it have to be Callie? She'd be about as helpful as an umbrella full of holes.

Still, Callie knew Geneva and Carmel. Maybe she'd seen them tonight.

"You young people!" the woman called cheerfully as Abby approached the counter. "Out on a night like this. Both you girls ought to have your heads examined."

Abby shook rain from her cape and swiped at her face with a tissue. She asked the owners if they had seen her sisters, describing them.

"Hasn't been much of anybody in here tonight," the man said. "We planned to close early, but decided there ought to be at least one drugstore open on a night like this. We live upstairs, so there's no place we have to get to before the flooding hits. Guess we'll be safe enough up there."

Abby turned to Callie. "You haven't seen Geneva and Carmel, have you?"

"I just got here. But no, I haven't. Why? Your mother would never let them out in this weather, would she?"

"My mother's not home. She's working. Moira was supposed to be in charge. I've called all the girls' friends. No one has seen them. I'm scared they might have come down here to watch the river rise."

"Oh, mercy," the woman declared, "I hope not. Won't be any time at all till that river's jumped its banks."

"It already has." Abby gestured with one hand. "Below the bridge, just south of the intersection out there. I could see it from the corner. Looks like a lake. Hasn't crossed the intersection yet, though."

The man thought for a minute, then said, "You'd best find those sisters of yours. Callie, you go with her. You're a good swimmer. Lord knows, you've come in here enough times waving a newspaper picture of yourself with a swimming trophy. I'd come along, too, but I don't swim. Never did learn. Neither did Susan here." He asked Abby then if she wanted them to call Search and Rescue.

The suggestion horrified Abby. She wasn't going to need such extraordinary help, was she? Wasn't she just going to find her sisters watching the river from a safe distance? Wasn't she going to yell at them until her throat was sore, and then take them home? After that, she'd hurry back to Med Center to see how Sid was doing. That was the way the scenario had unfolded in her mind. This man was suggesting something very different. "No," she said sharply, beginning to back away from the counter. "No, thanks. Callie, are you coming?" Having Callie along was better than going back out there all alone.

Callie looked surprised. "Oh. Yeah, I guess so. It's not like I have anything better to do." She glanced down at the small white bag in her hands. "My mother doesn't need this stuff right this very second. Besides, I like Geneva."

"The only reason you like her," Abby said flatly as they left the store, "is, she's always doing things the rest of us don't dare do. Like climbing the water tower, and crossing the trestle on the railroad bridge, and talking back to her teachers.

She's been in more trouble than the other five of us combined. You're getting your kicks vicariously through my sister, Callie."

"I have to get them somewhere," Callie grumbled, reaching up with one hand to restrain the red hat that threatened to blow away in spite of the tie under her chin.

"You Susannah Grant?"

The voice startled Susannah. She was perched on a high stool near the nurses' station, busily scribbling patients' names on a small notepad in her lap. When she glanced up, she recognized the tall, thin boy in front of her, his face and hair wet, as Aaron Thompson, Kate's younger brother. She slid off the stool. "Yes, I am. And you're Kate's brother. I've seen pictures of you." She extended a hand. "Hi. Nice to meet you."

To her chagrin, he ignored her extended hand. "Where's my sister?" he asked abruptly, keeping his eyes focused on a point somewhere above her head.

Flushing, Susannah withdrew her hand. "She . . . she isn't here. She went to the library."

A gurney flew by. Susannah had a vague image of someone who looked as if she'd just been swimming. Sodden, long dark hair hung over the edge of the wheeled stretcher, dripping water onto the floor. Another narrow escape from floodwaters? The gurney disappeared into trauma room three.

"I have to go," she told Kate's brother. She waved a hand. "They might need me in there."

"My sister is supposed to be here," he said brusquely. "Where is she? I have to tell her we're not at the house. That she shouldn't go there. We've already left. They made us evacuate." His eyes flashed darkly, and Susannah sensed that he was angry about having to leave his house. He shrugged toward the door. "We're over there, at the Rehab building. Tell Kate to go there."

A group of nurses and doctors hurried by them. A nurse accidentally brushed against the arm of Aaron's wet jacket and, without turning around, automatically reached out to wipe her own arm dry. "Don't worry," he called softly after her, "the color doesn't rub off."

Oh, Susannah thought, he's like that, is he? Angry at more than just the evacuation. Kate wasn't like that. If she was, she hid it well. Which was a possibility, Susannah supposed. "I told you, Kate isn't here. She left. She had a paper to work on, so she went to the library. As far as I know, she's still there."

His eyes narrowed suspiciously. "How'd she get there? In this weather?"

"My brother took her. He was going . . . somewhere." Susannah felt foolish, being unwilling to admit to this boy she didn't even know that her brother had ventured into the South Side of the city in spite of imminent flooding. "So he gave Kate a lift."

"He's taking her home, too?"

"Oh. No, I . . . he was on his way somewhere. I guess she was going to take the shuttle home." Susannah remembered Jeremy then. "But . . . a friend of ours went looking for her. He'll probably give her a ride home. I wouldn't worry about her."

He looked at her then. "No, I don't guess you would. Why should you?"

Annoyed, Susannah drew herself up to her full height. "Because she's my friend," she said heatedly. "But I'm sure she's okay." She paused, then added, "I'm sorry you had to leave your home. I don't blame you for being upset. I would be, too."

He laughed. There was no humor in the sound. "Like that's something you'd ever have to worry about. I *know* where you live. Way up there on that hill, high and dry, so far above everybody else. What's that feel like, anyway?"

"High and dry," Susannah answered curtly. Without saying that it had been nice meeting him, because it hadn't, she turned on her heel and left.

At the library, Kate slammed a book shut and uncurled her legs from underneath her, stretching them out before lowering her feet to the floor.

They landed in water. Very cold, and very wet. She was wearing black flats. Water spilled over the edges of the shoes and into her knee-highs.

Her eyes flew to the floor. It was covered with half an inch of dark, muddy water.

"Oh, no!" Kate jumped from her chair, wincing as her feet squished. "How . . . ?"

She couldn't believe that water had entered the building and snaked its way down the hall and into her little cubicle without her noticing. But the only light in the room was a small desk lamp on her table. There was no light at all out in the hallway. She'd been engrossed in her research, and the water hadn't made any noise. It wasn't rushing, wasn't bumping into chair or table legs with a loud thumping noise. It had seeped into the building quietly, sneaking up on her.

Kate stood in the middle of the small cubicle, gazing around her with wide, astonished eyes, then looking down again at the pool in which she stood. "This," she said aloud, "is not good. This is not good *at all*."

At the fishing lodge on the South Side, the party was in full swing. The music was loud, the crowd in good spirits in spite of the howling of the wind outside. People were eating and drinking and talking and laughing and dancing, as if it were just an ordinary party on an ordinary night.

But because it wasn't an ordinary night, the party's host wasn't doing any of the things his guests were doing. Because it wasn't an ordinary night, he was standing at one of the wide picture windows overlooking the river, watching silently as the Revere climbed steadily to the second of the three terraces, as if it had every intention of joining the party.

There was only one more terrace to go. Above that was a short but steep slope planted with shrubbery held in place by railroad ties, and then the first-floor veranda. Those were the only obstacles between the rapidly advancing river and the fishing lodge.

At the rate it's rising, Sam told himself grimly, all of that will be swallowed up in no time. Unless it stops raining. If it stops raining, the river will go down quickly.

If it didn't . . .

To keep that grim possibility out of his mind, Sam turned away from the window and rejoined his guests.

During a momentary lull in the steady stream of gurneys arriving at ER, Will and Susannah were sipping hot coffee in the lounge when Kate's mother, Astrid Thompson, poked her head into the room. "Since my family and I have been relocated temporarily to Rehab," she said cheerfully, "I decided to volunteer my services over here." She grinned. "So convenient, being right next door. Don't have to take a bus. Not that I'd want to take up permanent residency at Rehab. Anyway, my husband and my son have left for a sandbag crew, so here I am. What do you need?"

"How many hours do you have to spare?" Will asked dryly.

Nurse Thompson laughed. "I figured. That's why I'm here. I remember the last flood. Wasn't just near-drownings that kept us going. We had just about every injury you could think of. Bumps, bruises, lacerations, heart attacks, concussions, you name it, it was all there. And we were short-staffed at the same time. Not a pleasant experience, I can tell you. Where's Kate? In a treatment room?"

Susannah and Will exchanged a reluctant glance. He was the one to say, "She's not here."

Nurse Thompson had been leaning against the door frame. As Will's answer to her question registered, she stood up straight, her eyes dark with concern. "Not here? She has to be here! She didn't come home for dinner, and she didn't call. When I checked the phones and realized the lines were down in Eastridge, I just figured she'd decided to stay here where she was needed but

101

hadn't been able to call to tell me." Looking at Susannah, she asked, "If she's not here, where is she?"

"She had to go to the library. But," Susannah added hastily, "she left before the roads got too bad. So I'm sure she got there okay. And Jeremy went over there to give her a ride home." She didn't add that she'd been worried ever since Jeremy left that the library might have closed early and he wouldn't find Kate there.

"The library?" Astrid frowned. She was an attractive woman, tall and thin like her daughter. Susannah admired and respected her, and was grateful for the support the nurse had given her from the moment she had first begun volunteering. "The library's in the middle of town, and it's not up on high ground like Med Center. It'll flood, like it did the last time. How long ago did Jeremy go after Kate?"

Susannah and Will said they didn't remember exactly, but she knew they were both thinking the same thing. By the time Jeremy went to get Kate, the library had probably already taken on some water. It was very possible that Kate had left the building.

What troubled Susannah about that possibility was, Kate would have realized almost immediately, when she saw the streets flowing with water, that she wouldn't be able to get back to Eastridge. She would then have changed her mind and returned instead to Med Center.

But she hadn't shown up. Not yet.

So where *was* she?

At the library, Kate slipped out of her wet flats. Carrying them in her hands, she sloshed out of the room and down the hall to the back-door.

It was locked. From the outside.

She remembered, then, reports in the newspaper about recent break-ins. Nothing had been stolen, but there had been some vandalism. The librarian must have decided to take additional safety measures as a result of those incidents.

He'd picked a fine time to get cautious. How was she supposed to get out?

You're not supposed to be *in* here in the first place, she reminded herself. If he'd known you were down here, maybe he would have unlocked the door for you. You should have spoken up when he yelled down the stairs.

Too late now.

Kate peered out through the glass door window into nothing but darkness. The rest of the world had disappeared. Maybe it *floated* away, she thought with an uneasy giggle.

"No problem," she said aloud, turning away from the door. "I'll just go upstairs, find an extra set of keys, and go out the front door."

The water in the hallway was cold, her knee-highs little protection. By the time she reached the stairs and hurried up them, she was feeling chilled. She sat down on the top step to shed the sodden knee-highs and rub her feet dry with the edge of her maroon sweatshirt. Then she jumped up and hurried in her bare feet to the semicircular desk in the center of the main room, where she knew keys were kept on a hook beside one of the computers. She'd seen them when she was checking out books. There were several small lights still burning, probably another security measure. She was grateful she wouldn't have to hunt in the dark.

The keys weren't there.

The only thing hanging on the hook now was a small plastic card bearing the emergency telephone numbers of police, fire, and Search and Rescue.

Might come in handy, Kate thought dryly. *I might need those numbers if I can't find the keys.*

She moved around behind the desk to begin her search.

In the staff lounge, the conversation between Astrid Thompson and Susannah and Will was abruptly interrupted by a loud, urgent shout from outside the room.

"My boy! Where's my boy!" a deep, anguished voice called out. The shout was followed by

loud, crashing sounds, and then more shouting. *"My boy, my boy, I want to see my boy!"* There was such raw pain in the voice, it was blood-chilling to all who heard it.

Astrid Thompson whirled and ran. Susannah and Will followed, with the two nurses and the orderly dropping their coffee cups and exiting right behind them.

chapter

9

The group led by Nurse Thompson arrived in the ER lobby to find a huge, burly man with a reddish beard and thick, fierce eyebrows, his beefy face scarlet with rage, in the process of lifting the wheeled steel cart filled with patient charts. The seams of his red-and-black-checked flannel shirt strained as he bodily lifted the cart and tossed it against the wall. Charts flew everywhere. Some landed on the nurses' desk, knocking pens and pencils and a clock to the floor; some hit the walls so hard, they left dents in the pale yellow wallboard. Most fell to the floor and skidded crazily.

The man continued to shout, his words slightly slurred. *"You bring me my son, you hear me? You bring him to me, right now! I'll take care of him, don't you worry about that, I can take care of my own son!"*

The cart disposed of, the bearlike man lumbered toward his next target, a wooden table loaded with magazines, sitting between two blue plastic chairs.

"Has anyone called security?" Astrid Thompson asked of a young, white-faced nurse standing behind the desk now littered with charts.

The girl nodded silently. "They said it might be a few minutes. They're all downstairs checking out the emergency generator." She paused, her wide, frightened eyes never leaving the rampaging man, then added, "He said his name is Brock. I think he's been drinking."

"Oh, God," Susannah cried softly, "his son just died! Curtis. He was trapped in the river in his car. But it wasn't a drowning. Dr. Lincoln thinks he panicked and had a heart attack. He . . . he was only sixteen." She turned to Will and the orderly, standing slightly behind her. "We have to do something! Before he hurts himself or somebody else."

"*What have you done to my son?*" the man screamed. He lifted the table high above his head, the magazines slipping and sliding off the edge. Then he heaved it. People watching in horror from the wide doorway of the waiting room cried out as the table flew through the air straight toward them. Some dove out of the way, some hid their faces against the wall as if not seeing would protect them, others fell to the floor and covered their heads.

The table crashed to the floor, splintering into a dozen pieces of shattered wood. A thin slice of wood landed in the hair of a woman in a plaid dress standing with her face pressed into the wall. A longer shard penetrated the fleshy upper arm of a man lying on the floor. He cried out in pain and shock. A third chunk hit a teenaged boy just below the left knee, buckling it and sending him to the floor.

"What have you done to my boy?"

Before Susannah could stop him, Will broke away from the group and slowly, carefully, but very deliberately, approached the man, speaking in a calm, quiet voice. "Sir, you don't want to do this. You've hurt some people here, people who didn't have anything to do with what happened to your son, okay? If you'll just calm down, someone will come and talk to you about the boy, explain what happened. Could you just calm down, sir? You don't want anybody else to get hurt."

Susannah held her breath. Will was tall and strong. An athlete. But the man possessed twice Will's bulk, and his rage was an awesome thing to witness. "Will," she breathed, "be careful."

The man glared at Will with reddened eyes. *"You know what they did?"* he cried, his bearded mouth twisting in pain. *"They killed my boy! They said his heart stopped! Then they sent someone to the refinery, a cop, a cop I didn't even know, a stranger, to tell me my boy was dead!"*

Will laid a hand on the man's arm. Susannah froze. If that arm came up and swatted at Will with the full force of the man's unbridled anger . . .

"I am really sorry about your son, sir," Will said. "I know how you must be feeling. How about if we go into the lounge over there and I get you some coffee and we'll talk about your boy? Would that be okay?"

Security arrived at that moment, a man and a woman in Med Center's tan uniforms. They would have moved toward the man, but Astrid Thompson put up a hand, signaling to them to hold off.

"You know about my boy?" the man asked Will. All of the anger seemed to have left him. Susannah saw tears gathering in the red-rimmed eyes. "You knew my Curtis? He was my only kid, you know."

"No, I'm afraid I didn't know him, Mr. Brock. But I would like you to tell me about him. Over here, in the lounge?" Gently, making no sudden moves, Will led the man, docile now, out of the lobby and into the lounge. The two security officers followed.

Sam knew he should do something.

The road leading from the cabin to the main highway was at the foot of the slope, where the third terrace began. If it didn't stop raining and if the river continued to rise, that road would become impassable. *Soon.* And there was no other road out. He didn't mind spending the night in the cabin if the entire slope flooded. But he had to let everyone else know what was happening.

He turned away from the window and moved through the crowd to the stereo to switch it off. The music ended so abruptly, it startled everyone into silence, making it easier for Sam to make his announcement. He stepped up onto the wide, stone fireplace hearth and addressed his friends in his normal, hearty tone of voice. "Listen up, everyone! Sorry about interrupting the festivities, but I think it's only fair to warn you that if we don't leave soon, we might not be able to leave at all. The old Revere is climbing the walls out there . . . and I mean that literally. It's up to the second terrace. When it reaches the third, we'll need a boat to make it back to town. The road out of here will be an Olympic-sized swimming pool."

"So?" one of Sam's soccer teammates spoke up.

"You've got boats, right, Grant? Didn't I see a boathouse out there?"

"The only way anyone could get to that boathouse now," Sam replied, "would be to swim. The river has it surrounded. Look, I'm staying here, but anyone who'd rather beat a hasty retreat right now won't get any flak from me, okay? It's probably the smart thing to do. All I'm saying is, if you intend to go back to town tonight, you'd better do it right now." When no one said anything, he added, "If you're *not* leaving, and you parked anywhere below that third terrace, you'd better go out and haul your car up here closer to the cabin before it becomes amphibious."

The party guests divided quickly into two groups: those who were staying and those who weren't willing to risk it. Most thought it was wise to leave, although no one really wanted to. Some couples argued, one partner wanting to stay, the other determined to leave. One girl became so incensed, she stomped from the cabin without her date. Sam thought he recovered very quickly, gravitating toward a girl whose date had also left. They consoled each other by calling the deserters "wimps."

Sam didn't agree. There were six people left,

including himself and Becka, and he found himself wishing they had all chosen to leave. This party had been *his* idea, and they were in his cabin. That made him responsible for them on a night when Mother Nature was in charge, not Samuel Grant III.

He was just about to turn to the remaining party guests and try to convince them to leave, when a brilliant streak of lightning lit up the windows, a resounding crack of thunder shook the lodge, and all of the lights went out.

Sid Costello awoke again, this time with a start, his heart pounding in his chest. The room was completely shrouded in a black-velvet darkness. The small half-moon of light that usually shone beneath his door from the hallway was gone. He turned his head toward the window. He was on the fifth floor, too high up to see any light from below. But on every other night since they'd brought him to this room, there had been outside that window the reflected glow of the complex's walkway lamps, a pale but constant illumination that Sid had found reassuring, as if the faint cloud of yellow was telling him, yes, life is still going on out here and we expect you to rejoin us soon.

That glow was gone now. There was nothing

but unbroken darkness outside his window, as if someone had hung a thick, black drape over the glass.

Maybe someone had. Maybe the nurse who had found him with the window open had put it there. To keep him inside.

That wouldn't explain why the hallway outside his room was also pitch-black.

Sid fumbled for the buzzer to summon a nurse. He couldn't find it. He hadn't been taking his nighttime medication, and had been sleeping restlessly. If the cord to the buzzer hadn't been looped tightly over the bed rail, he might have dislodged it in his sleep, maybe even knocked it to the floor.

Well, I'll just jump out of bed and pick it up, he thought giddily. And laughed aloud, a harsh sound in the silent room.

Another clap of thunder sounded as lightning lit up the window.

Sid got it then. No one had hung anything over his window. The electricity was out, that was all. So why bother hunting for the buzzer? Wasn't it electric? It wouldn't work, anyway, not until the emergency generator came on.

The door opened and a nurse with a flashlight hurried over to his bed. It was the same nurse who had found him at the window. "Oh, you're awake," she said when she reached him. "Didn't you take your sleeping pill?" Her face was a disapproving yellow moon above the flashlight. "Not hoarding them, are you? Where are they, under your pillow?"

It annoyed him that she was assuming he was suicidal just because he was paralyzed. Wasn't she also assuming then that his life must no longer be worth living? Who did she think she was to decide that? He'd make that decision himself. When he was ready. He wasn't ready yet.

Before she could begin fishing around under his pillow for the pills, he shook his head and pointed to the drawer on his bedside table. "I'm not hoarding anything. I just don't want them anymore. They make me too groggy in the morning." He didn't add that if he wanted to do something as stupid as take his own life, collecting enough sleeping pills to do the job would take too long. The window was faster and surer. Provided he could figure out how to hoist himself up over the sill from a wheelchair. But he still thought of that as a coward's way out. "What's with the lights?"

"They'll be on in a minute." She opened the drawer, collected the half-dozen pills, and pocketed them. "Dr. Davids will have to hear about this."

Davids. The shrink. So? Why would a shrink care if a patient takes his sleeping pills or not? "Why aren't the lights on now?" Sid asked angrily. "Doesn't your emergency generator come on automatically? This *is* supposed to be a modern facility, isn't it? My parents are paying a small fortune so that I can lie here in the dark?"

"Your parents aren't paying anything. The insurance company is. And I told you, the lights will be on in a sec. There seems to be some little glitch with the emergency equipment."

Some little glitch. She said it so casually, as if it were totally unimportant, because after all, she wasn't lying here in this bed in total darkness, was she? She had a flashlight, and she could turn and walk out of the room and close the door and go back to other people with flashlights. She could go back to the outside world and be normal, but he couldn't. He had to stay here, in this black hole, by himself, knowing that if a real emergency came, he wouldn't be able to save himself. Scary thought. Very scary thought.

"I want O'Connor," he said flatly. "Now! Get that stupid flashlight out of my face and get O'Connor for me."

The nurse stared down at him. "O'Connor? We don't have a Dr. O'Connor on staff."

"She's not a doctor, you dimwit!" He was

shouting now, waving his arms at her. "She's a volunteer! Abby O'Connor! Call her and tell her to come over here!"

The nurse was dumbfounded. The flashlight wavered in her hand. "A volunteer? Now? It's too late . . . it's too nasty out there . . . I can't . . ."

"Yes, you can!" Sid tried, and failed, to sit up straighter, hoping for the appearance of authority. Instead, he slid further down on the pillow. That made him even more furious. He could feel his heart pounding like the drums he played in his rock band, and his hands were shaking with fury. "Call her at home! Tell her it's me, tell her it's an emergency. Just get her over here! Or I'll . . ."

The nurse didn't say, "Or you'll do what?" But Sid himself thought it, and that sickening feeling of total helplessness that he'd been fighting so hard to squelch swept over him. Or what? What was he going to do if the nurse refused to call Abby? Jump out of bed and race for the door? Hike all the way home? Steal a bicycle and pump the pedals until he was at his own front door?

"Please," he said quietly, looking away from her. "Please call Abby."

The nurse hesitated only a moment. She directed the flashlight away from his face, and said just as quietly, "Okay, I will. I'll call her."

116

She was halfway to the door when she turned, walked back to the bed, and thrust the flashlight at him. "Here. You keep this. I'll get another." Then she left.

Even without the light, he would have been grateful to her. Because she hadn't said, "Or you'll do what?"

The flashlight helped calm him down. He held it tightly in one hand, letting its beam illuminate the doorway so that when Abby came in, he'd see her clearly.

In downtown Grant, Abby and Callie struggled, side by side, along Massachusetts Avenue in water up to their knees. The riverbank, underwater now, was to their left, the darkened stores and restaurants on their right. The avenue itself had disappeared, swallowed up by the swollen Revere.

"This is dangerous!" Callie shouted above the wind. "This water is moving too fast! And there isn't anybody around to help us if we get caught up in the current. I'm barely staying on my feet!"

"That's because you're wearing stupid high-heel boots!" Abby called back. "Who goes on a rescue mission in high-heeled boots?"

"When I left my house, I didn't *know* I was going on a rescue mission, did I?" Callie grabbed at the branches of a semisubmerged shrub for support. "You should have warned me in advance that your sisters were going to do something this dumb."

"Dumb? Dumb? You're the one who said you liked Geneva!"

"That was then. This is now." A sudden gust of wind ripped Callie's wide-brimmed red hat off her head, in spite of the ties beneath her chin. The ties gave, and the hat sailed away, landing upside down in the muddy water and rushing away amid a sea of debris. "Damn! I loved that hat! And my hair . . . look, Abby," Callie shouted, "I am soaked through to the bone, I'm going to drown any minute now, my toes are so wet, they're probably going to have to be amputated at Med Center, so no, I don't like your sister anymore, not one tiny little bit. When we find her, I'll be the one to strangle her, not you. I'm going to do it with my bare hands. If I have any strength left."

Abby clutched the top of a parking meter whose pole had disappeared beneath floodwater. She had to gasp her answer, but she managed to pack a certain amount of smugness into it.

"I knew you'd change your mind about Geneva," she said.

—∿∿∿∿∿∿∿—

The emergency generator had kicked in quickly, providing adequate light and the use of all electronic medical equipment, to the relief of the staff.

When the patients who had been injured in Mr. Brock's rampage had been treated, Susannah returned to telephone duty. There were fewer calls now, which she realized had to be due to lines being down in other parts of the city. That made her uneasy. If the phones went out at Med Center, too, how would people call for help? Were there, even now, people stranded or injured out there who hadn't been able to get to a working telephone?

There was a phone at the fishing lodge. The library, too, had telephones. But neither Sam nor Kate had called. Were those phones out?

"No, ma'am," she told an anxious mother who called, "I don't see your daughter's name on my list. She's probably at a friend's house, waiting out the storm." She hung up, hoping the daughter hadn't been one of those brought in without identification. There had been quite a few, although the pace had slowed somewhat. People were finally getting the message and staying indoors.

Will was about to join a crew on an ambulance run when Nurse Thompson stopped him.

"No, Will," she said firmly. "You've already put in your hours. You must be exhausted. I want you to rest."

"How can I rest? I haven't heard from anyone in my family, have you, Susannah? My mom and brothers weren't brought in while I was in the lounge with Brock, were they?" His tone was light, but Susannah heard an underlying anxiety.

If I had family in Eastridge, she thought, I'd be worried, too. My family is safe at the top of a very high hill. Except for Sam, of course.

"No. I'd have told you if anyone from your family came in. I'd have interrupted you and Brock, who, by the way, you were brilliant with, Will." Susannah smiled at him. "How did you stay so calm? The rest of us were quaking in our shoes."

He shrugged. "The man wasn't drunk. He was in pain. I guess he wanted someone else to feel it."

"But you're the only one who did."

Another shrug.

"I'm sure your mother and the boys are safe," Nurse Thompson told Will. "You might want to check at Rehab on your way out. See if they're over there yet. Now go on, get out of here. Dr. Lincoln will take care of Mr. Brock, so you can leave. Scoot! That's an order."

"See you later, Will," Susannah said, knowing the nurse was right, but still sorry to see Will go.

"Oh, no, you don't!" Nurse Thompson said. "What I told Will goes for you, too, Susannah. You've been here almost as long as he has. Go home and get your beauty sleep."

"But . . ."

"No buts. I know it's been horrendous here tonight, but we've got staff coming on at eleven. Go home. Your parents must be worried about you."

"No, they're not. I called and told them I was staying here." Her mother hadn't mentioned Sam, and neither had Susannah. She could only assume he'd called home and said that everything was fine. She hoped. Not that her mother would have asked *her* about Sam. Her parents knew that she and her twin led very different social lives. Susannah hardly ever knew exactly which party or dance Sam was attending, or which girl he had chosen to honor with his presence.

When Nurse Thompson had returned to her desk, Susannah said to Will, "I can't go home and sit around doing nothing while the city is flooding. I'd never be able to sleep."

Will nodded. "I'm with you. But orders are

orders." They began walking toward the door. The crowd in the waiting room had thinned some. Those who remained, still shaken by the episode with the angry Brock, sat quietly watching the weather channel on television. As Susannah and Will passed, one man jumped to his feet and approached them.

"I just want to shake your hand," he said to Will, extending his own hand. "If you hadn't calmed that man down, Lord only knows what would have happened. You're a very brave young man. Thanks."

Susannah smiled at Will's obvious discomfort. But he shook the man's hand and made a hasty statement in support of the grieving father.

Outside, they were reluctant to dash out into the steady downpour. They stood on the top step under an overhang. "I feel so guilty about leaving," Susannah said, hugging her arms around her chest against the wind. "The weather hasn't improved at all. The staff is going to be up to its elbows in patients all night long."

"Astrid's right, though. We're burned out, Susannah. People make mistakes when they're tired. We could send a cardiac patient to the Psych ward or vice versa." Will zipped up his navy windbreaker. "You said you brought the Benz?"

Susannah had to raise her voice to be heard above the sound of water smacking against the cement steps. "Yes! Do you need a lift?"

"No, but *you* do. You can't drive that. It sits too close to the ground. I've got my truck. I'll take you home."

Susannah loved the idea of being alone in Will's truck with him. But she knew how tired he was. He should go find his family, and then get some rest. "West Grant won't be flooded. I'll be okay. That car handles like a dream, even on slippery roads."

"Don't argue with me. I know your part of town doesn't flood. But you have to get there from here. You could hit high water almost anywhere. You're coming with me. You'll be as safe as if you were in a tank."

"An amphibious one, I hope." Will took her hand and they ran down the steps and across the spongy grass to the parking garage.

When they were inside the truck and on their way out the long, wide, tree-lined driveway, he said, "Tell you what. Neither one of us wants to leave, right? Maybe all we need is a quick break. Why don't we go somewhere and grab coffee, maybe a doughnut or a piece of pie, see how we feel then? Anyway" — he glanced over at her with a grin — "by the time we get back, maybe Astrid will be back at Rehab. A new night nurse won't know how long we've been there, right? How about it?"

"Great!" The trees along the driveway were bending double under the force of the wind. The truck splashed through deep puddles, sending cascades of water against the windows and windshield. "*If* any of the night staff can get to the hospital."

"Yeah, well, there is that. But it's worth a try." Then he concentrated on steering the truck through the sea of swirling black water. Susannah glanced at his handsome profile and smiled. In spite of the weather, she felt safe with Will at the wheel.

Kate couldn't locate any extra library keys. They weren't on the desk anywhere, and the desk drawers were all locked. Maybe, as another precautionary measure, the librarian had taken all of the keys home with him, so that if someone did break in, they wouldn't have easy access to the drawers.

Like they couldn't break into the drawers the same way they'd broken into the building!

Irritated, her feet cold, her ears attuned to the sound of water lapping hungrily at the basement stairs, Kate lifted the telephone on the desk to call for help. She had her fingers already poised to dial when the unmistakable sound of dead air greeted her.

Kate replaced the receiver. Her irritation was quickly replaced with real disappointment. She had planned to call Med Center, talk to Will, ask him to come and get her in his truck. No problem. She knew he'd do it willingly. And he'd find a way to get a library door open. Will was smart and resourceful. Now she couldn't even call him.

The disappointment was just as quickly replaced by a sensation Kate quickly recognized as uneasiness. She had no key, no way out of the building, and the water in the basement was rising rapidly. This was trouble, no doubt about it.

She stood at the desk in her cold, bare feet, glancing around the room with narrowed eyes. Okay, so she was *not* going to be using the telephone to summon help. The world outside had not only disappeared from sight, it had disappeared from *sound,* too. Her one link to voices in other, safer places was gone.

She was alone. She was more alone than she had ever been before. This was nothing like spending a night alone in the small yellow house when her parents had gone to the Berkshires for a well-deserved minivacation, and Aaron spent the night at a friend's house. Those nights were fun. Pretending that she lived alone in the house, watching whatever she wanted on television, playing her stereo at full blast, eating whenever and whatever she liked, staying up late, spending hours on the phone with friends. She hadn't been lonely for a second. Besides, she'd had Lancelot, the family English springer spaniel, who loved to sit at her feet with his head and long, matted ears in her lap.

Feeling uncertain, a feeling Kate definitely wasn't used to and found almost more frightening than her circumstances, she sank into the desk chair and tucked her feet up underneath her in an effort to warm them. She knew she had to do something. She just wasn't sure what that something was.

The only coffee shop still open in the area was a diner with worn red plastic booths and a pattern of muddy footprints across the black tile floor. The waitress, the sole employee, had scattered short, fat candles across the counter and on the tables, and had substituted an old-fashioned coffeepot on the gas stove for the electric coffeemaker. The candlelight was kind to the worn surroundings. There were no other customers.

The coffee smelled wonderful, and the pecan pie sitting on the counter in a glass case looked delicious.

It was. And the waitress was very friendly. "I live in Eastridge," she said as she poured coffee for Susannah and Will. "They just said on the radio that they're not letting anybody back into that area now. It's being evacuated. Everyone's being taken to the Rehab Center. I think maybe I'll just sleep here tonight. Might even keep the place open. That way, rescue crews and the like can stop in and load up on caffeine if they want."

When she had left them alone, Will looked so bleak, Susannah said, "You should probably go straight to Rehab when we get back. You must want to be with your family."

"It's not that. They'll be okay. My mother will see to that. It's the thought of the cleanup afterward. I remember it from last time. It was really putrid. The mud clings to everything. It gets in the cupboards, the closets, the drawers. All of our family photo albums were wrecked. That hit my mother hard. And all the bleach in the world won't make that smell go away until it's good and ready. Takes forever."

Susannah pictured her beautiful three-room suite at the top of Linden Hall covered with foul-smelling mud, and shuddered. "I guess I'd want to move."

It was an innocent comment, sympathetically delivered, but Will's face tightened. "I guess you would. That wouldn't be a problem for your family, would it? Your parents could just buy another mansion somewhere else in town and fill it with brand-new furniture and rugs and drapes. No one in Eastridge has that luxury."

"I know that," she said quietly. "I didn't mean . . ."

He waved a hand. "Forget it. That wasn't fair. It's just . . . I get a little ticked sometimes because Eastridge always seems to get hit the hardest with floods, the refinery fires, that kind of stuff. Like I said, most of the people there can't afford to live anywhere else in town."

Uncomfortable, Susannah sipped her coffee silently. Outside, the storm continued unabated. There was almost no traffic now, although during their twenty minutes in the diner, three ambulances, two fire trucks, and two police cars raced by.

"I'm not going to live there all my life," Will added emphatically. "But I *am* going to work with the people there. A clinic, I think. Maybe in that big, old red brick building on East Sixth, the one that used to be a theater before it was closed down? That'd make a great clinic. When I'm a practicing physician." His lean, handsome face cleared, and he laughed. "Ever wonder why they call it a practice? Don't doctors ever get it right?"

"You will." Susannah smiled. "You'll get it right. And," she added boldly, "you'll need another doctor working there with you, won't you? In your clinic? Keep me in mind, okay?"

He plunked his coffee cup down on the table. Unlike her smile, his was cynical. "Oh, sure, Susannah. There probably isn't anything in the world your father would rather see you do than work in some shabby little clinic on the east side."

Her own smile widened into an impish grin. "It doesn't have to be shabby. We'll get my mother to decorate. She's an expert, and I can talk her into donating her services."

Will shook his head, but he was laughing. When his laughter died, he said seriously, "You'd really consider it? Working in a clinic with me?"

"I think I'd love it," she said just as seriously.

Impulsively, he reached out and covered her hand with his. "Well, I'd like it, too."

The door opened and Jeremy Barlow burst into the diner. He stopped abruptly, just inside the door, as he took in what he was seeing.

Will's face closed off and he withdrew his hand. "Hey, Barlow," he said casually, leaning back in the booth, "what are you doing out on a night like this?"

"Looking for Kate." Jeremy slid into the booth beside Susannah. "She's supposed to be at the library. But I drove by there, and it was closed. There were a few lights on, but it looked totally deserted. She couldn't have been in there."

"Well, at least the electricity isn't off in that part of the city, like it is here," Susannah said. "Not yet, anyway. But I wonder where Kate went? She wasn't at Med Center. Unless she went straight to Rehab looking for her family."

Jeremy frowned. "I don't see how she could have gone to Med Center from the library on her own. I had a hard time navigating. On foot would have been worse. The streets over there are starting to flood. Looked like there was already water in the library's basement."

"Probably was." Will stood up. "It flooded last time. Lost a lot of books, some of them rare. Kate must have left when the water started coming into the basement. If she was doing research, she'd have been down there. Would have seen it right away."

"Will's right," Susannah added, standing up, too. "But Kate wouldn't have gone home, even if she could get there. She'd know Eastridge was about to be evacuated. I'll bet anything she's at Rehab. We're going back there now, Jeremy. Why don't you come, too, check it out?"

Jeremy nodded. "Right. Let me grab a cup of coffee to go. I'll be along in a sec. But," he added grimly as Susannah and Will left, "she'd better be there."

Kate had just begun her search for the keys when the electricity went out. Every last ray of light disappeared, both inside the building and out. Everything around her had been erased in one swift stroke. She couldn't even see the floor beneath her feet. She stood perfectly still, her mouth open in surprise.

"Well!" she said finally, disgust in her voice, "isn't *this* exactly what I need!"

11

The temperature began to drop drastically. Neither Abby's nor Callie's raincoat was lined, and both were so thoroughly drenched, they no longer provided even a hint of warmth. Both girls were shivering, their teeth chattering as they continued to slog through the deep water covering Massachusetts Avenue. Although they were not more than a few blocks from the public library, the avenue lights were still on, and they could see the river continuing to rise and swell, spreading out to snake its way under the doors of the closed shops and restaurants on their right.

"Abby, this is totally crazy!" Callie shouted. "This water may only be up to *your* thighs, but I'm shorter than you. It's up to my waist. I can't keep walking through this. The current's too strong. Can't we just go to the police and make them look for your stupid sisters? That's their job!"

"It would take too long," Abby called back through a jaw clenched with cold. "You go if you want. They're not *your* sisters. You can bring the police back with you, or a rescue crew. They must be around somewhere. But I'm going to keep going. I know Geneva and Carmel have to be down here, and I'm going to find them if it kills me."

"It just might," Callie said grimly. But she didn't leave. She wasn't sure why. She knew she was not particularly brave. Privileged and pampered all of her life, there'd been little need for bravery. The closest she'd come until now was the courage it took to drive her chronically ill mother to Med Center three times a week for dialysis, a painful procedure necessary to do the job her mother's kidneys could no longer perform. That took courage on the part of mother and daughter alike. But Callie didn't think of that as bravery. She thought of it as necessity.

Now, she wanted nothing more than to turn around and go home to her nice, dry, warm, luxurious house, completely safe from muddy floodwaters. She would take a long, hot shower and put on her best silk pajamas, the peach pair her father had brought her back from Hong Kong. She would put her newest CD on and crawl into bed to get warm. But first, she'd give her mother the bottle of medication that she had tucked into her blouse chest pocket to keep safe and dry.

Abby had *said* it was okay for her to leave. So why wasn't she leaving?

She knew why. She wanted Abby O'Connor

132

to *like* her. That's why she wasn't leaving.

What puzzled Callie about Abby was, of all the people Callie knew, Abby seemed the happiest. And Abby had the least. Oh, she had a nice enough house, and her family owned two cars, a station wagon and a van. But they weren't *rich*, like practically every other girl Callie knew. Abby lived in a perfectly ordinary house in a perfectly ordinary neighborhood and went to perfectly ordinary Grant High instead of private day school. Abby had a big, noisy family and tons of friends and she smiled a lot, even though she lived such a perfectly ordinary life. Why was it that Abby smiled so much more often than Callie Matthews? Why did she date more than Callie did? And why did she have so many more friends? When she was so . . . *ordinary*?

And why did Callie want someone so ordinary to like her? So much so that she was risking her very life trying to help Abby O'Connor find her stupid sisters?

Callie didn't have the answer to those questions. All she knew was that she didn't want to turn around and leave Abby out here all alone in the middle of an avenue that had become a tributary of the Revere River.

Gritting her teeth, Callie plunged onward.

Susannah and Will, with Jeremy right behind them, went directly to Rehab when they arrived back at Med Center. Will wanted to check on his family, and Susannah had picked up on Jeremy's anxiety about Kate. What if she wasn't at Rehab? They knew she couldn't still be at the flooding library, and she couldn't have gone home to Eastridge. What if she'd begun to walk home in the storm and had been caught up in heavy floodwater somewhere in the city?

Did Kate swim? Did she swim *well?* Susannah didn't know.

If Kate wasn't at Rehab with her family, they would have to check with the rescue teams to see if her name was on any of the lists of rescued flood victims. Beyond that, Susannah had no idea how they'd go about locating Kate.

There was a large, handmade sign tacked onto the wall beside the entrance to Rehab, a wide, low building some distance behind Grant Memorial. Susannah guessed that when the sign had first been hung, it had read FLOOD SHELTER. But the ink used hadn't been waterproof, and the letters had begun to drip down the sign in black rivulets. It now read F O D ELT R.

Inside, the building looked very different. The main lobby, decorated with leather furniture, expensive leather-topped tables which Susannah knew her mother had picked out, and huge pots of fresh flowers, was mobbed with people receiving name tags and filling out forms. Will, intent on finding his family, and Susannah, equally intent on locating Kate, pushed their way through the crowd and into the main room on the first floor. The huge space, which Abby liked to call "The Ballroom," although as far as Susannah knew, nothing as formal as a ball had ever been held there, was bustling with activity. The floor was a landscape of cots and bedding spread out across its shiny hardwood surface. People sat or lay on the makeshift beds. The few belongings they'd managed to bring with them were piled at their feet. The faces of the adults, most of whom were women, registered confusion or anger or shock, while the older children looked interested in this exciting change in their normal routine. The very young children were perfectly happy anywhere as long as their mothers were with them. Their fathers were out working on the sandbag crews.

There was no sign of Kate.

But her brother, Aaron, was standing in the middle of the room. Susannah spotted the tall, thin boy who had confronted her earlier in ER, and was torn. She didn't want to ask Aaron Thompson about his sister. He'd probably bite her head off. But how else could she find out if Kate's family had heard from her?

She was spared the question when Aaron moved over to her and asked, "Have you seen Kate?"

Susannah shook her head. "No. And I'm worried. Although," she added quickly, "I know she can take care of herself."

"Are you sure?" he asked rudely, and walked off. His face was filled with concern.

Susannah wondered what to do next. She was standing alone, her eyes searching the crowded room for someone else who might have seen Kate, when a deep voice behind her asked, "Aren't you a friend of O'Connor's?"

Susannah turned around. The boy in the wheelchair was almost as good-looking as Will. Same strong face, high cheekbones, and keen, intelligent eyes, although these eyes were not as warm as Will's. And they were blue, not dark brown. The hair was dark brown, and the mouth had an unpleasant downturn to it, which Susannah guessed probably had something to do with the wheelchair. "You mean Abby?"

"Abby, yeah. Abby O'Connor. I think I've seen you here with her."

"She's my best friend. You know Abby?"

He shrugged. "Yeah, I know her. She's my volunteer."

Susannah raised an eyebrow. *His* volunteer? Volunteers weren't supposed to become attached, emotionally or otherwise, to any of the patients. They'd been warned about that. Had Abby disobeyed? Not likely. Besides, she hadn't mentioned anyone special at Rehab. "What's your name?"

"Sid Costello."

The name registered with a shock. Susannah recognized him, then. She remembered the stories and his picture in the newspaper and on television when he'd fallen from the water tower. Everyone in town had been interested because everyone in town knew who Sid Costello was. He looked very different now from those pictures. They had been of a tall, strong, healthy football player in a Grant High uniform. His smile had been a little arrogant, she'd thought at the time. Maybe a *lot* arrogant. This Sid, wearing a bright red V-necked sweater over a white T-shirt, his legs covered with a plaid blanket, wasn't smiling at all, and didn't look as if he would be anytime soon.

"Where is she?" he demanded.

"Abby? She went home."

"I know *that*. But I told the nurse to get her back here. She said she would. That was more than an hour ago. I finally got tired of waiting in my room. Too noisy to sleep, with all the doors slamming down here, and people yelling. I could hear it five floors up." He glanced around the room as Susannah had. "I thought O'Connor might be down here, doing her do-gooder thing. She's still at home?"

"I guess so." Abby had never once mentioned Sid Costello to Susannah. She must not be as interested in this guy as he seemed to be in her. If

137

she wasn't interested, it certainly wouldn't be because of the wheelchair. Not Abby. If she really liked a guy, he could have paws instead of feet and she wouldn't care.

But the guy would have to be really likeable. Sid Costello didn't seem to qualify. "Is there anything I can get you?" Susannah asked politely. "Since Abby's not here, I mean. Did you need her to do something?"

He looked her up and down with thinly disguised contempt. "You mean since I can't do things for myself?"

Susannah's cheeks burned. "No, I . . ."

"I just want to see her, that's all. You know her number?"

"Of course I know her number," she snapped. "I told you, she's my best friend." She'd met lots of people in wheelchairs while volunteering. None of them had been as rude and unpleasant as this boy. Maybe he thought that just because he was in a wheelchair, he deserved special treatment and didn't need to be civil to people. That wasn't what the volunteers had been taught in their training.

"Don't coddle them," Astrid Thompson had warned them. "You will have to make allowances for their physical challenges, of course. But other than that, you must treat them as you would any other human being. They deserve that. They're entitled to it. Getting nothing but sympathy would do them no good at all."

"If Abby's home," Susannah said more matter-of-factly, "she's probably very busy. Taking care of her brothers and sisters. She might not have time to talk on the phone."

"Just give me the number, okay? If she doesn't want to talk, fine. I can deal with that. But that's up to her, not you."

She gave him the number and stalked away. She was going to have a talk with Abby about this Costello boy. Weird that Abby hadn't mentioned him. He wasn't exactly forgettable.

Having made sure that his family was safe, Will was ready to leave with her and return to ER. Jeremy decided to return to the library. His face looked very strained as he left.

"Maybe Astrid won't let us back in," Susannah told Will as they left Rehab. "We were ordered off the premises, remember? For the safety of the patients, I believe we were told."

Will glanced at his watch. "It's after eleven. The new staff's probably on duty by now. And if Astrid got stubborn and didn't leave and won't let down the drawbridge for us, we'll come back over here. They could use help here, too."

It occurred to Susannah as they hurried through the enclosed passageway from Rehab to ER that every hospital on the grounds of Med

Center could probably use extra help tonight, since all of them would almost certainly be short-staffed due to the weather. Will was right. If they weren't allowed back into ER, they wouldn't have any trouble finding somewhere else to volunteer.

But she knew that ER, as always, was where she really wanted to be.

When the lights suddenly went out at the fishing cabin, there were startled cries as the six remaining occupants reacted to the sudden darkness.

But what Sam decided was worse than the darkness inside was the loss of the outside floodlights. With the storm continuing, he would have liked to send everyone back to their own homes. He could have talked them into leaving. He'd talked them into coming down here, hadn't he? But unless he found a couple of flashlights or lanterns, he couldn't let anyone step one foot outside the cabin now, because there was no way to see how high the water had risen.

"Sam?" Becka's voice was shaking. He knew she hated the dark. Still slept with a night-light on, she had told him in a rare moment of openness. Most of the time, it was impossible to figure out what Becka was thinking. No problem figuring out what she was thinking now. She was scared. "Sam, where *are* you?"

He reached out a searching hand. His fingers connected with hers. They were clammy and cold. "Sam, do something!"

"Come with me." His own voice was firm, steady. Deliberately so. "I know where the flashlights are. Don't let go of my hand."

"Don't worry, I won't!"

Leading the frightened girl, Sam cautiously made his way to a cupboard beside the fireplace, pulled a drawer open, and unearthed a large flashlight. He could tell by its feel that it was the black one his father often carried on nighttime visits to the boathouse. Wondering when it last had new batteries, Sam flicked it on. The beam was orange-yellow, and it was very strong.

Beside him, Becka breathed a sigh of relief, and her grip on his hand eased a little. But just a little.

Sam played the flashlight's beam on the other party guests, clustered together now in a tight little group in the center of the room. The sudden darkness had rendered all of them, even Joel Mitchum, the practical joker in the room, silent. No one said, "Hey, Sam, it's okay, no big deal!"

"Sam," Becka said, her voice hushed, "I want to go home. Now. Please."

Sam turned slightly toward her. He didn't know how to tell her there was no way that could happen now. Even if they could somehow get away from the cabin in spite of the water surrounding it, the lights were probably out all across the city, and the Revere was on its worst rampage in years. There would be no highway lights, no working traffic signals, only car headlights to see if the road being traveled was underwater. By the time those headlights illuminated a deep lake spreading out in front of a vehicle, it could be too late to turn back.

Complete darkness and flooding were a lethal combination.

Wishing fervently that he had listened to Susannah hours earlier, Sam began awkwardly, "Listen, Becka, the thing is . . ."

The new night nurse in ER was regaling the staff with tales of her journey through the storm when Will and Susannah returned. Nurse Thompson was absent, although one of the nurses said she was still on duty, but had gone upstairs on an errand. Lost in her story of trees uprooted by the wind, and deep, torrential streams washing the roads she'd traveled to Med Center, the new nurse took no notice when the two arrived.

They hung their jackets on the rack in the staff lounge, signed in, and when Susannah had donned her pink smock, they went out into the lobby. Will moved quickly to the chart cart, restored to order after Brock's attack on it, and casually began leafing through the charts.

"Look at this!" He waved one in the air. "Nine patients while we were gone! Nine!" He glanced over at the staff gathered around the night nurse. "We must be having a lull. Temporary, though, I'll bet." He replaced the chart. "Most of the incoming were people pulled out of the river or low-water crossings. Minor bumps and bruises, that kind of thing. Couple of car wrecks. Nothing critical." He shook his head. "Can you believe there are people out in this?"

Susannah smiled. "Will, we were just out in it."

He laughed. "Yeah, but *I* know what I'm doing. Lived here all my life. I know which roads to take and which ones to avoid during flooding. Anyway, the diner was just up the road."

"Yeah, but you didn't know when we left here that it would be open, did you?"

He donned a look of mock ferocity. "Are you trying to pick a fight with me? If that one hadn't been open, I'd have taken only certain, very safe streets to find another place." He had a very serious expression on his face now. "I would never take any chances with you in the car, Susannah."

She knew that was true. Still, it felt nice to hear him say it aloud.

"Anyway, my point was," Will said, clearly wanting to change the subject, "they've been busy here, Doesn't look like it's going to ease up anytime soon. The storm *or* the inflow of patients. I'm glad we came back."

"Me, too." Almost as an afterthought, Susannah asked, "Do you know Sid Costello?"

Will nodded. "He's a friend of mine. I go to Grant High too, remember? We're . . . we were on the same football team. I stop in to see him whenever I can. Some of the people at Rehab think he's not handling this business very well. But nobody ever says what handling it well means. Is he supposed to smile and say, 'Hey, this isn't so bad after all'?"

"I don't know what handling it well means. Anyway, he seemed awfully anxious to get in touch with Abby. I didn't even know she knew him. I should call her, let her know he wants to talk to her. Just in case he wasn't able to get through."

A voice barked over the PA system. Incoming. A car had hit a telephone pole. The pole had fallen on top of the car. Three patients, all critical. ETA seven minutes.

"If you're going to call her," Will told Susannah, "you'd better get to it. In seven minutes, this place is going to be too noisy to hold a telephone conversation."

Susannah ran to the desk and dialed Abby's number.

"Oh, Susannah," Moira wailed into the phone, "Abby isn't here! She went out looking for Geneva and Carmel, and she never came back!"

chapter
12

It was the sound of the water lapping nearby that awakened Kate. Still seated in the librarian's chair, she had fallen asleep. It took her several moments to realize where she was. The library was so still and silent, she could hear her own breath. The only other sound was the smacking of the encroaching water upon the wooden stairs, and it was that sound that caught her attention. It was too close. Much closer than it should have been.

Kate pulled herself upright in the chair, her eyes searching the darkness. She couldn't believe she had fallen asleep. I must have been more tired than I thought, she decided, peering around her. All that studying . . .

If only she could see. She would have given anything for a candle, a flashlight, a lantern. Anything to break this thick black curtain and take away her feeling of helplessness. How could she do anything useful if she couldn't *see*?

It wasn't the darkness she was frightened of. It was the water, so stubborn, so persistent, climb-

145

ing ever higher. Without a light, how could she tell how close it was getting?

She remembered, too late, that the library had been flooded more than once in the past. Which made it not the best place to be trapped in on a night like this one.

Kate stood up. She was stiff from sleeping in the chair. Her muscles ached. How could she have forgotten that the library had been flooded previously? If she'd remembered, would she have come here, anyway? Probably. For one thing, she would never have expected the water to rise so quickly. She would have been positive that she could finish her work and beat a hasty retreat while the building was still dry.

Exploring the darkness with her hands and stepping cautiously, Kate made her way slowly to the top of the stairs. Stepped down one step. Dry. Stepped down another. Still dry. But the sound of the water slapping persistently against the steps was louder now. She imagined it calling to her, saying slyly, "Come on in, the water's fine." Down another step. This time, her bare foot landed on wood that felt damp and slick. Not yet fully engulfed, but about to be.

She calculated quickly in her head. There had been, she thought, nine or ten steps leading up from the basement. Only the top two were still dry. The step below them was about to be swallowed up. The basement hallway below was completely lost to her now. Underwater. Her only hope of exit was the front door. If she could get it open.

She tried. She tugged and pulled on the door-knob, kicked the door with her bare feet, pounded on it until her fists felt raw. But it didn't budge. Kate couldn't believe that vandals had ever gained entry to this place. To her, the library seemed locked up tighter than a fortress.

Although there was no full second floor to the building, there was, she knew, a small loft at the top of a set of six wide, wooden steps off to one side behind the librarian's desk. The loft was a small, private, quiet reading area filled with bookshelves and two comfortable old chairs, each with a small lamp table.

And . . . wasn't there a long, narrow window up there looking out over the street? If she could get that window open, she could shout for help.

That would only work, she knew, *if* there was another human being within miles, which, given the weather, there probably wasn't.

But it was worth a try. Kate stifled an ironic laugh. Like she had a choice? Window or not, there was only one place for her to go to escape the rising water, and that was *up*. The loft wasn't very *far* up, but it was all she had.

Searching with her hands again, Kate moved toward the staircase.

* * *

The victims of the car wreck and the utility pole arrived at the ER in a flurry of activity. All were teenagers.

"They probably thought it would be a lark to drive on flooded streets," Dr. Izbecki grumbled as the three gurneys arrived, one after the other. But after that initial complaint, he settled down to begin the business of saving lives.

One patient, a boy Susannah didn't recognize, had no pulse and wasn't breathing. The second patient, a girl whose short, spiked black hair was streaked with blood, had a severe head injury, while the third, a younger girl, had a critical chest injury.

"No seat belts," one of the paramedics announced unnecessarily. It was already obvious to the medical professionals that seat belts had not been used. The injuries were too severe.

Each patient was directed to a different trauma room. Susannah decided she would be of more use in the room with the chest injury. And that girl was so young; if she regained consciousness, she'd be frightened.

The girl with the head injury was wearing a cervical collar and lying on a backboard, measures taken at the accident site to prevent further injury. She, too, was unconscious, but the wound on the back of her skull had stopped bleeding. The paramedic pushing her wheeled cart snapped, "She's in a bad way. Unresponsive.

Pupils unequal. Blood pressure's in the basement, seventy over fifty. There wasn't much we could do for her in the field. She's all yours. Lots of luck!" He sounded depressed.

Susannah, running alongside the second gurney, overheard. Severe head injury. Not good. The patient might not die . . . Dr. Izbecki could probably save her with his initial efforts, and then the neurosurgeons would take over. Med Center surgeons were the best in the world. But sometimes there was only so much they could do. The girl might never again be the person she was when she'd climbed into that car earlier in the evening. Even if there was no permanent brain damage, she would probably have to learn to walk and talk all over again, as if she were an infant. The recuperative period would be long and painful.

Of the chest injury patient, the paramedic said, a bit breathlessly, "We've been pouring fluids into her, but we got nothing. BP was still low. So we applied the antishock trousers."

"I advised against it on the radio," Dr. Izbecki snapped. "The last thing we need in a chest injury is an increase in pressure in the girl's chest. The trousers could have done that. You could have killed her."

The paramedic frowned. "We knew the risks. But giving her fluids did zilch for blood pressure. We thought it was necessary."

His partner added, a bit defensively, "We were watching her. At the first sign of respiratory distress, we would have deflated the trousers."

"Never mind," the doctor said brusquely, "just get her into the trauma room. And somebody get me X Ray, stat!"

Susannah ran to the phone and made the call.

She learned later that the boy who hadn't been breathing when he was brought in was the driver of the vehicle. After what Will described to Susannah as a tense, lengthy period of resuscitation attempts by Dr. Lincoln, he had revived, with no signs of brain damage from a lack of oxygen. Both his legs were broken, one suffering a compound fracture, and he had a serious eye injury.

"He's also facing reckless driving charges," Will added, standing beside Susannah as she finished gathering up towels in the trauma room. "The officer on the scene said they can do that because of the warnings that went out over television and radio. No one's supposed to be out on the roads. And that kid almost killed two other people. They're sisters, those girls. If they'd both died, their parents wouldn't have any daughters left at all."

"They'll live," Susannah said confidently. Both girls had been taken up to surgery and would be transferred to separate hospitals in the complex when they passed the critical period. "Dr. Izbecki was amazing with the chest injury. Fast and efficient, but so gentle. If I were going to work in Emergency Care, I'd want to be exactly like him."

"Well, as long as you don't *look* like him!"

Susannah laughed. Dr. Izbecki was not the most handsome doctor on staff. His face was rugged and weathered, as if he'd spent too many hours in the sun. She knew that wasn't true, because the man hardly ever left the hospital. Someone had told her he'd grown up very poor, in Chicago, and hadn't had it easy. Maybe that was what she saw in his face. Handsome or not, he was still her hero. He had saved a twelve-year-old girl's life, and as the girl had been wheeled off to surgery, one of the other doctors in the room had said in admiration, "Great work, Jonah! I didn't think you'd pull it off. Not this time." And Dr. Izbecki had said only, in his usual gruff tone, "That's what we're here for." Then he'd stripped off his rubber gloves and hurried off to see how the patient was doing.

"I'm going over to Rehab to see if Abby is there yet," Susannah told Will when she had tossed the towels into the laundry bin. "Moira said she went looking for Geneva and Carmel. But I can't believe she's out in this. I don't *want* to believe she's out in this! Maybe she found them and instead of taking them home, decided all three of them could help out at Rehab."

"Carmel's only eight, Susannah," Will said.

"Do you really think Abby would expect her to volunteer? Carmel isn't even big enough to push a wheelchair."

"She could maybe answer phones or something," Susannah said stubbornly. Her eyes pleaded with Will. "I'll be right back."

"We might need you here."

Susannah was exhausted, and her uneasiness about Abby was growing. "Well, it's not like I'm a nurse or doctor," Susannah said testily. She waved a hand toward the staff, some of whom were just emerging from a trauma room. "You've got *plenty* of help. I said I'd be right back. Okay?" Without waiting for a response, she hurried off in the direction of the enclosed passageway leading to Rehab.

"This is Sid Costello," he said into the telephone. "I'd like to speak to Abby, please." He was sitting at a pay telephone in the lobby of Rehab, surrounded by throngs of people waiting to make calls on one of the six phones. They crowded around him, impatient. He found himself wishing for the privacy of a booth, even though he knew a booth would be inaccessible to his wheelchair. Rehab had freestanding phones for wheelchair patients. He had chosen not to use the phone in his room because he'd been afraid a nurse would barge into his room while he was talking, and afterward she'd ask all kinds of stupid questions about "the girl in his life." Gag. He couldn't deal with that.

It was impossible to hear. There was a great deal of static on the line, and the lobby was so noisy with so many people in it. He'd never seen the place this packed. He could barely make out the voice that finally answered. "What did you say? You didn't say she wasn't home, did you?" He'd been so sure that all he had to do was pick up a phone and she'd be there, on the other end of the line. "Are you sure? She left here a long time ago. She was supposed to be going home. Where else would she be?"

Crackle, crackle, snap, on the line. "She's out" . . . crackle, crackle, snap . . . "for . . . sisters . . ." crackle, snap, crackle. It was hopeless. All he could gather from the garbled conversation was that Abby was not home.

Then even the crackling snap disappeared. The line went dead.

"Sorry," Sid said as he handed the telephone to the person behind him, an older man with anxious eyes, "it's not working anymore." The man glared at Sid as if it were his fault.

Sid wheeled himself over to the elevator. He punched the button. But before the doors slid open, the girl with long, blonde hair, the one he'd talked to earlier because she was a close friend of Abby's . . . best friend, she'd said . . . came hurrying down the hall, calling his name.

He couldn't believe how glad he was to see her. She'd know where Abby was.

But she didn't. "Have you seen Abby?" were the first words out of her mouth.

Sid let the elevator doors open and close again without him. He turned his wheelchair so that he was facing Susannah. "I just called her house. I think I was told that she wasn't home, but I can't be sure. The line was a mess, and then it went dead. Why?"

"Because she *isn't* home. Moira, that's her sister, said Abby had gone out looking for her two younger sisters, and hadn't come back yet. I was hoping they were all here. You haven't seen them?"

Sid shook his head.

Susannah surveyed the lobby. Then she moved around behind Sid's chair to begin pushing him toward The Ballroom.

"What are you doing?" he cried over his shoulder. "I don't want to go in there! It's packed with people. I was on my way to my room when you showed up. Take me back to the elevator!"

Susannah continued to push the chair. She leaned over his shoulder. "You were going to go up and hide in your room with all this going on down here? Why aren't you helping?"

"Helping? Me?" His laugh was scornful. "Oh, man, I'd be a big help, wouldn't I? I'll bet all of the other volunteers are wishing like mad that I'd offer my services. Probably bitterly disappointed that I haven't."

"Well, you still can. There are plenty of things you can do to help. You can ride this chariot to the linen closet and bring back towels and blankets. You can answer phones."

"I told you, they're not working."

"Well, you can take names from people here then, and the phone numbers of their relatives. Then, when the phones are working again, you can call them and tell them their family members are here. There's plenty of work here for someone even as cantankerous as you."

Cantankerous? An old-fashioned word. But Sid knew what it meant. It meant cranky, difficult, even rude. He'd thought she was going to say "crippled" or even "physically disadvantaged." Cantankerous wasn't so bad.

Susannah steered the wheelchair into the wide open doorway to The Ballroom, her eyes quickly scanning the crowd. "Darn, she's not here! Oh, God, Sid, do you really think Abby is out in that storm somewhere?"

The look he sent her then was full of suspicion. Instead of pitying him, she was dumping her worry on his shoulders, as if she expected him to know what to do with it. As if he could make *her* feel better. She was talking to him the same way she would to anyone, as if he were an ordinary person. Was this some new form of therapy? Or was she so worried about her best friend that she'd forgotten whom she was talking to?

Still, he sat up straighter in his chair. And he found himself wanting to reassure her. He didn't know what to say. He wasn't used to people asking him for something. All he could come up with was, "I don't know if she's out there. But . . . but I sure hope she isn't."

He knew it wasn't enough. Susannah's face didn't suddenly relax; her eyes, which were a really bright blue, didn't look relieved. He felt like he had let her down. Hating the feeling, he felt compelled to add with fake enthusiasm, "Okay, if you insist, I guess I could go get some blankets or pillows or something. Just until O'Connor shows up, though, okay? Then I'm outa here."

Susannah looked down at him. "You think she'll come here?"

"Oh, yeah, sure." He forced a grin, the cocky grin he'd worn in the pictures in the newspaper. It wasn't easy. He hadn't used it in a long time. But it finally appeared on his face. "How could she stay away, when *I'm* here?"

"Oh, you are *so* full of it!"

But Sid thought, as Susannah began pushing his chair toward the linen closet, that she looked a little less worried.

chapter
13

At the fishing lodge on the South Side, Sam returned to the window overlooking the Revere. Becka had unearthed a bunch of candles from the cupboard beside the fireplace, and the first-floor living room danced with flickering flames. But that didn't help illuminate anything outside. Without the floodlights, it was impossible to see how high the water had risen in the past few hours. They'd been sitting inside, alternately partying halfheartedly and sleeping, for what seemed like days. But it wasn't days. Sam's watch informed him that it was one-thirty in the morning. His parents wouldn't be frantic yet. But soon.

He didn't have to *see* the river to know how high it was. He knew how bad the situation had become. All this time, he deliberately hadn't opened the front or back door to check, because he didn't *want* to see. What difference did it make how high the water had risen? They couldn't leave, anyway. It was better not to know.

Still, his curiosity was getting the better of

him. Anyway, sooner or later, he was going to have to step outside to see if his foot landed on something solid, or floated. Might as well get it over with.

He waited until the other five were engaged in a heated discussion about who really *was* the sexiest man in the movies (Becka taking the position that it definitely wasn't Brad Pitt), before moving quietly to the front door, opening it, and stepping onto the porch.

His foot landed on wet, but not submerged, wood.

This was good.

But when he moved across the porch and stepped down one step, his foot was instantly soaked.

Oh, man! The *top* step?

Everything below that top step was underwater.

At the rate the water was rising, it would be only minutes before the Revere River inched its way into the living room where his friends were arguing.

He had no choice. He would have to move the party upstairs. And he'd better have a really good explanation for insisting they leave the perfectly comfortable living room with the big stone fireplace and the oh-so-excellent stereo system, and move upstairs to a floor that housed only bedrooms.

Sam *knew* what the explanation had to be. He would have to tell them the truth.

Will, standing just inside the ER entrance as a car screeched to a halt in the driveway, found himself wishing Susannah would return. They couldn't possibly need her as much at Rehab as she was needed at ER. Following the three teenagers whose car had been creamed by a telephone pole, there had been two near-drowning victims, rescued from floodwaters, a six-year-old child who had fallen from a ladder while being evacuated from the second story of his house in Eastridge, two cardiac arrests, and two teenaged boys who had thought it would be a blast to take a raft down the raging Revere. They had collided with the stone bridge in the center of town.

Those two cases had been the worst. One critical head injury, similar to the girl in the utility-poled car, and one near drowning. Both victims were still teetering on the edge upstairs in Intensive Care. They were both lucky to be alive. If they weren't in the best ICU facility in the country, they wouldn't stand a chance.

Since the two cardiacs, one of whom, a retired postman, hadn't made it, things had quieted down some. But Will knew it wouldn't last. In the meantime, there were reports to be filled out, supplies to restock, frantic relatives in the waiting room to placate. How many times tonight had a nurse or doctor said (voice rising a little each time the standard quote was repeated), "I assure you, we're doing the best we can"? He'd said it himself when an anxious relative in the waiting room waylaid him as he ran by to greet an ambulance and help rush a patient to a treatment room.

Susannah was better at that than he was. She had what he called The Perfect Patient Touch, and it applied to relatives of patients, as well. A calm, soothing voice, never condescending or impatient, combined with the ability to listen to even the most trivial complaints without losing her temper. She *would* be a valuable asset to his clinic. But her parents would never allow it. Never! Before the ink was even dry on her medical license, Samuel Grant would have Susannah set up in a lucrative private practice somewhere up near Linden Hill.

She *had* sounded interested, though. Probably just being polite. She'd probably never even been *in* Eastridge. Parts of it were nice enough. Other parts weren't. They'd get all kinds of people in his clinic. And while there wasn't a snobbish or intolerant bone in Susannah's body as far as he could tell, was she really prepared for what they might see at the clinic?

The car that had screeched to a halt, an older-model sedan, still had its lights on, glowing eerily through the sheets of rain. A door opened, a woman in shorts and a T-shirt jumped out, ran to the passenger's door, reached in and plucked something from the seat, turned, and ran through the rain up the sidewalk. Will yanked the door open for her.

She was carrying a small child, wrapped in a blanket. The woman was crying hysterically, lines of black mascara streaking her face. "Help me!" she cried when she saw Will. "You have to help me!"

Will signaled to a doctor and nurse in the lounge. They jumped up and hurried toward him. "What happened?" he asked, taking the limp child from its mother's arms. She didn't want to let go, and continued to clutch at one edge of the sodden blanket as Will turned and began moving down the hallway. The child, who looked to be around two or three years old, lay as limp as a rag doll in his arms. Its eyes were closed, the lids bluish, its mouth open.

"I thought he was asleep," she cried. "In his room. But when I went up to check, he wasn't there. I couldn't believe his bed was empty! I don't know how he got by me. I was just sitting in the living room, watching the late movie. He must have come downstairs and slipped right past me. The doorway is behind the couch."

Patiently, Will repeated, "What happened?"

The woman let go of the blanket to swipe at the wet hair hanging in her eyes. "He got out of the house, he does that sometimes if I forget to lock the door after I put him down for the night. He got out!" She clearly still didn't believe it. "I found him" — she choked on her tears, stopped, tried again — "I found him in the drainage ditch in front of our house. Floating. It was overflowing, because of the rain, and I found him *floating*!"

With the doctor and nurse alongside them, they reached a trauma room. Dr. Izbecki was inside, waiting. Although his manner was rough, Will trusted him completely with children. He was always very gentle with them. And he would know what to do for a child this small.

"If a big branch hadn't been blocking the culvert," the woman finished as Will carefully laid the child on the table, "he . . . he would have floated away, the water was rushing so fast. It was trying so hard to push him right through the sewer pipe, but the branch wouldn't let go of him. That's what that scratch on his cheek is from. If it hadn't been for that branch, he would have kept going, just disappeared, yanked off to . . . to the river. I never would have found him in time!" Her voice trembled with terror as she reached out to clutch at the child's limp right hand, hanging over the edge of the table. "I did find him in time, didn't I?" When no one answered her, her voice rose. "*Tell* me I found him in time!"

Instead of answering, the nurse asked quietly, "What's his name?"

"What? Oh. His name is Louis. Louie. For my husband. He's out of town. He was supposed to be back tonight, but the weather got so bad, his flight was canceled." Her voice broke. "Oh, God, how am I going to tell him I forgot to lock the door? He'll blame me, he will! He keeps saying three-year-olds don't go out of the house in the dark alone, but Louie does, he does, I don't know why, he just does. . . ."

The nurse did her best to persuade the young mother away from the table, but to no avail. Will knew Susannah could have done it, and felt a wash of anger. Why wasn't she here, where she belonged, when they needed her? He couldn't even remember what had been important enough to drag her away from ER. Something about Abby.

"Why didn't *my* electricity go out?" the young mother wailed. "Driving over here, I saw lots of houses that were dark, and the streetlights were out. If mine had gone out, too, I wouldn't have been watching the late movie, and maybe I would have checked on Louie sooner!"

"Get her out of here!" Dr. Izbecki snapped as he and his colleagues began working on the child. "Give her a sedative. I'll sign the order. All we need now is for her to go into shock on us. Do it, okay?"

Everyone in ER joked about Dr. Izbecki, "His bark is worse than his bedside manner, but not by much." Will respected the man. He knew what he was doing, and what he was doing right now was trying to save the woman's child. For that, he needed her calm and out of the way.

The mother, whose name was Edie Murphy, refused the sedative until Dr. Izbecki, already beginning resuscitation efforts on her child, told her sternly that without it, she would have to be removed from the room. As he worked, he ordered equipment. One nurse reached for an oxygen mask, another reached for a small needle to take blood, while a third ran for the portable chest X ray standing against a wall.

Taking seriously the threat to have her removed from the room, the toddler's mother submitted to the small blue pill one of the nurses handed her. She calmed down almost immediately and was allowed to stay.

Will knew the pill couldn't have worked that quickly, but for some people, just the idea of having taken a sedative calmed them down instantly, before the medicine could possibly have taken effect. He was grateful that this was evidently the case with Mrs. Murphy.

"No pulse, and he's apneic," Dr. Izbecki announced grimly as he worked on the small, limp form. "Let's get going here! We need to bring this one back."

Easier said than done, Will thought to himself. He knew the baby's chances weren't good. Everyone in the room knew it . . . except maybe Edie Murphy. She might not know that *apneic* meant he wasn't breathing. Small children almost always fall into water with their mouths open, filling their lungs very quickly. The child's chances, if he had any, depended on how long he'd been in that ditch before his mother found him.

If Louie died, this woman would never forgive herself. It would be futile to tell her that she hadn't killed her child, the storm had. She'd never believe that. Her husband might not forgive her, either. Will knew that even strong, healthy marriages were often destroyed by the death of a child, compounding the tragedy.

Will also knew you had to be careful administering CPR to a child as small as this one. The risk of tiny ribs breaking under the pressure of chest compressions was greater than with a full-sized teenager or adult. But for all his gruffness, Dr. Izbecki was incredibly gentle.

There was almost total silence in the room as the effort to save the baby's life continued. Other sirens came and went, but everyone stayed where they were. They had a child to revive.

Two more doctors, whom Will recognized as a pediatrician and a cardiopulmonary specialist, arrived and stood by silently, waiting to see if they would be needed. Word of new emergencies traveled fast at Grant Memorial.

"Please, please, please," Edie Murphy breathed, her clenched fists to her mouth, her eyes never leaving the table, "please don't take him from me!"

Will swallowed hard and silently echoed the word *please.*

"We've got a pulse," the nurse announced excitedly. "It's thready, but it's there."

Will knew that Mrs. Murphy was waiting for something dramatic to happen then, like Louie beginning to cough and then maybe cry, to prove that he was back among the living. It wasn't going to happen that way, if it happened at all. They might get a pulse, and he might even begin to breathe on his own . . . although he probably wouldn't, not right away . . . but he wasn't going to sit up and smile at his mom. No television program with a happy ending in thirty minutes here. When they'd finished emergency treatment, he'd be carted off to Pediatric ICU, probably hooked up to a whole bunch of monitors, more wires and tubes in him than a television set. Even then, they wouldn't know for a couple of days if he was going to be okay.

Then Dr. Izbecki said, "Well, all right!" and, heaving a sigh of relief, stood up straight. "This little one is among the living. Get him upstairs, stat! And tell them up there that I want

166

an hourly update, you got that?"

"Yessir," the nurse said. She was smiling.

"He's okay?" Mrs. Murphy cried, taking a step forward. "He's going to be all right?"

Will couldn't stomach watching her face fall again when Dr. Izbecki bluntly explained the dangers still ahead for Edie Murphy's small son, so he offered to escort the gurney upstairs, along with the nurse. No one argued with him.

Behind him, as he left the room pushing the still-limp form on the white, wheeled table, he heard Dr. Izbecki begin, "Mrs. Murphy, I need you to understand what I'm about to say, so please listen carefully."

But . . . at least the baby was still alive. Everyone in ER would be keeping their fingers crossed for him. That should help.

"That was rough," the nurse said, looking down at the boy with compassion in her eyes. "Think he'll make it?"

The elevator arrived, and Will held the door while she pushed the cart inside. "Yes," he said firmly as the door closed, "I do. I think Louie here is going to grow up just fine and live to hear his mother telling stories about how he wandered around at night like a baby vampire when he was only three. That's what I believe."

That was what he *wanted* to believe.

He was still annoyed with Susannah for not being there, for not going through this with him.

What was she doing all this time over at Rehab, anyway?

What Susannah was doing at Rehab was trying to reassure Jeremy Barlow that Kate Thompson was safe.

"I tried to get back to the library again," he'd said when he located her near the linen closet. "I couldn't get there. That whole area is flooding fast. Some of the streets are blocked off. So if she's not there, where *is* she?"

"Wherever she is, I'm sure she's fine. You know Kate. Who can take care of herself better than Kate can?"

"On a night like this?" Jeremy shook his head. His wavy blonde hair was very wet, and drops of water cascaded to the floor. "*Nobody* can take care of themselves in that storm! I was just over in ER, looking for you. I'll bet all those people they're bringing in by ambulance thought they could take care of themselves, too. Thought they could drive through high water, thought they could raft down the Revere, thought they were better and stronger than any dumb old storm." Jeremy's face was reddening.

"Hey, take it easy, man!" Sid called, turning his wheelchair to face the worried boy. "I know Kate Thompson. She goes to my school. She's vice president of our class, and that's because she's organized and efficient. Our friend here is right," waving a hand toward Susannah, who realized with a jolt that he probably didn't remember her name. "You don't need to worry about Kate Thompson." He astonished Susannah by smiling. "No storm is safe around Kate."

Jeremy didn't look convinced.

chapter
14

Although Kate was slender, she was very strong. She had on occasion pushed gurneys carrying patients who weighed twice what she did, and often hefted heavy loads of clean linen from one part of the hospital to another. Nevertheless, she had a terrible time trying to open the long, narrow, floor-to-ceiling window at the top of the stairs leading to the library's small loft. Unlocking the latch had been no problem. But when she reached down, confident that in another minute she would be able to scream for help, she was dismayed to discover that the window was firmly stuck. It probably hadn't been opened in years, if ever.

"I have got" — she tugged and pulled — "to get" — more tugging, more yanking, on the wooden frame — "this window open!" Using all of her strength, she gave the lower pane of glass an angry tug, and it jerked upward half an inch. "Come on, come on!" she urged, renewing her efforts, "I can't scream for help through that little bit of space." As she pulled, she repeatedly glanced over her shoulder toward the foot of the stairs, not so far below her. Although she could see almost nothing in the flat darkness around her, she thought she sensed motion. The floor was moving? No, the floor couldn't be moving. This was a flood, not an earthquake.

But something *on* it was moving.

And Kate knew what that something had to be. Water. Already! In the space of the ten minutes that it had taken her to climb the stairs and wrestle with the window, the water from the basement had gobbled up the remaining two wooden steps leading from the basement and slid across the first floor like spilled syrup.

The window came up another five inches. Then, with an additional tug, it opened all the way to the upper pane of glass.

There were no new iron burglar bars up here as there were on the first floor. Kate stuck her head through the opening. Rain slapped against her face and hair, but she hardly felt it. She was concentrating instead on finding some sign of life out there in that thoroughly saturated world, some person she could call to for help. Even a dog would be better than nothing, because if she started screaming, maybe the dog would bark, and someone would come to find out what all the racket was about.

She was greeted by nothing but an eerie darkness made complete by the absence of streetlights

171

or any kind of illumination emanating from buildings in the area. When her eyes had become accustomed to the darkness, she could make out below her a swirling, muddy river, completely encompassing the building. She didn't need anyone to tell her that the water surrounding the library was rising steadily. What had happened in the basement was proof enough of that.

"I'm in the middle of the damn Revere River!" she cried out in disbelief. "You're supposed to be blocks away from here!" she shouted angrily. "What are you *doing* in this part of the city?"

Stupid girl, she chided mentally. You know perfectly well what it's doing. It's flooding, that's what! And you're stuck right in the middle of it. Because you had your feet up on a chair and weren't paying attention.

There was no point at all in screaming, she knew that. There was no one out there. Why would anybody in their right mind, which of course excluded *her*, be out on a night like this? All of Grant had probably been warned to stay inside their nice, safe, dry homes, and *they'd* paid attention.

She didn't know how to swim. She had never learned. There was no public pool in Eastridge, and traveling across town to the Y was too much of a hassle. If the building were on fire and flames were nipping at her heels, she'd have to jump to the ground and take her chances. It wasn't that high up. A story and a half. Maybe she'd break an ankle or a wrist when she hit the ground.

But there *was* no ground down there. Only water. Muddy, swirling, angry water. There was a gurgling sound below her. She looked down upon the wide, carpeted steps to her right. She couldn't be sure, but it seemed to her that the bottom step was now awash.

How could the water be rising so quickly?

"Stop *raining*!" she shouted out the window. "Stop it!"

The only answer she got was an angry gust of wind smacking her in the face so hard, she recoiled from the window in shock.

"I have to do something!" Jeremy insisted as he and Susannah walked back to ER.

"Well, just don't worry her family, okay? Her mother's on duty. At least, she was when I left ER. Don't say anything to her. Why don't you try the library again?"

"I told you, I can't *get* there! Besides, I thought we agreed that she couldn't be there. It's been closed since the first time I went over there. Unless she got locked in somehow, she's not there."

"Maybe she did."

The lights in the enclosed corridor, courtesy of the emergency generator, cast a sickly yellow pallor across Jeremy's face as he turned his head to

173

look at Susannah. "Maybe she did what?"

"Maybe she got locked in. You know how she is. I've studied with her once or twice. She disappears, totally, into any book she's reading. That could have happened, Jeremy." They rounded a corner, arriving at the glass door to ER. Susannah pulled it open. "There's a side door in the basement Kate sometimes uses. If she went inside that way, the librarian wouldn't even have known she was down there. And if she was concentrating the way she usually does, she might not have heard him leave. He could have locked her in accidentally."

"Finally!" Will exclaimed when he saw Susannah approaching. "Where have you been?"

"But I went over there," Jeremy argued. "It was pitch-black inside the library."

"The electricity could be out, Jeremy. That doesn't mean Kate's not *in* there! I think you should figure out a way to get over there and double-check." Susannah turned to Will to ask, "Kate's not here, is she? She didn't come in while I was gone?"

He shook his head no.

She turned back to Jeremy. "She's not here, and she's not at Rehab, and I don't know where else she could be. If she's in the library, and the whole area is flooded, she won't be able to get out. Not without help."

Jeremy looked dubious at the idea of *him* being the help Kate needed. So did Will. "I might be able to get through in my truck," Will said. "It rides pretty high off the ground."

Jeremy bristled. "I can do it myself. If I can't drive in, I'll swim in."

Will nodded. "Okay. I just thought I'd offer. I mean, we could go together. Like they say, two heads are better than one."

"I don't need you." To Susannah, Jeremy said, "I'll bring her back here. If I don't find her, I'll come back, anyway, so you'll know."

In spite of Will's obvious skepticism, Susannah believed that Jeremy *would* find Kate and bring her safely to Med Center. He had, after all, recently saved the life of a girl who'd been drowning in a private pool at a party in Susannah's neighborhood. Two football players had tossed the girl who, unknown to the boys, was in the first stages of the virus sweeping the city of Grant, into the pool. Then the boys had gone inside, not realizing that the girl was in trouble. Too weak and ill to save herself, she would have drowned if Jeremy hadn't arrived.

"What'd I say?" Will asked, a bewildered expression on his face when Jeremy, his back stiff, his jaw jutting forward with determination, had left the building.

"Nothing." Silently, Susannah wished Jeremy good luck. If he came back to ER without Kate, they would have to tell Astrid Thompson the bad news and see what she thought should be done to locate her daughter.

She had to admit that until Jeremy came back with Kate, every time a gurney came rushing in, she'd immediately look to see if the patient might be a tall, slender girl with dark, cornrowed hair, heavy wooden earrings dangling from her earlobes.

No, that couldn't happen. Kate would be okay. Kate could take care of herself.

As an ambulance pulled up in front of the entrance and Susannah joined Will in the familiar rush to the door, she hoped fervently that she was right.

Abby had almost no voice left. Although she continued to shout the names of her sisters as she and Callie struggled through the deep water covering Massachusetts Avenue, what came out of her mouth was little more than a hoarse croak. "We need a boat," she called across the water to Callie. The water was at Callie's waist, and Abby knew the girl couldn't go much farther. It was too dangerous. Callie weighed less than a hundred pounds. It was amazing that she'd managed to trek this far, with the current tugging viciously at her. "We need to give this up and go get some help. Maybe we can find a rescue crew somewhere around here."

"Abby! Abby, up here!" Geneva's voice came

not from the riverbed to their left, which Abby had dreaded, knowing it would be impossible to rescue anyone out there without a boat, but from somewhere ahead of them. Up? Geneva had shouted, "Up here!" Up where?

Abby raised her head, peering into the dark night. It was impossible to see. Every last bit of light had disappeared when the electricity blinked off some time ago. "Where are you, Geneva," Abby called.

"We're here, up in this tree!"

"Omigod, they climbed a tree!" Callie shouted. "They actually climbed a tree? Well, I'm not climbing any tree, Abigail O'Connor, I promise you that!"

A floating garbage can, metal and very large, slammed Abby in the small of her back. She would have fallen facedown into the water had there not been a parking meter to her right. She grabbed it and held on. The garbage can continued on its way. "Geneva? Keep shouting, so we can find you. We can't see a thing! Keep making noise. Sing or something."

There was moment or two of silence, then Geneva's deep, strong voice and Carmel's sweet soprano broke into a chorus of "Row, Row, Row Your Boat."

"So, what do we do when we find the tree they're in?" Callie asked, weakness and impatience in her voice.

"I'm going to kill them. We'll get them down out of the tree and then we'll drown them."

"Then what are we going to all this trouble for?" Callie grumbled. She was shaking with cold, her teeth chattering uncontrollably.

"Gently down the stream . . ."

Abby brushed a strand of thoroughly saturated hair from her eyes and glanced over at Callie. Most of the time, Callie was shallow, selfish, and spoiled. But if it weren't for Callie, Abby thought, trying to hurry, I'd be out here all alone. I don't even want to *think* about that. "Callie," she called, "in case I don't get a chance later, thanks. Thanks for . . . for being here."

"Life is but a dream. Row, row, row . . ."

"Right. Let's say you owe me, O'Connor. Let's say maybe you could think about getting me a date with one of those cute Grant High football players, okay?" Callie batted aside a pair of potted plants floating toward her. "You're a cheerleader. They're all your friends. They don't ask me out because I go to private school. See what you can do, okay? And we'll call it even."

Abby laughed, a laugh that got lost in the whistling of the wind, and thought, I should have known she'd want something. That's Callie.

"Gently down the stream . . ."

Then, suddenly, the singing voices were directly over their heads. They looked up. Carmel

178

was on the lowest branch, a thin limb that didn't look strong enough to hold her. Abby could barely make out Geneva's taller, heavier shape on the branch above Carmel.

"I'm going to kill both of you," she called up, trying to steady herself against the rushing water by hugging the tree trunk. "But first, you have to come down."

"I can't," Carmel said tremulously. "I'm too scared. Abby? I can't come down. You have to come up and get me."

Jeremy had driven as far as he dared. The moment he felt the wheels losing their grip on the road, he pulled over and parked on a slope, then set out on foot, flashlight in hand, toward the library. Taking side streets and shortcuts, he managed to avoid the most heavily flooded streets. Until he came to Market Street, two blocks north of the library. It was there that he had to begin wading in earnest.

He stood at the corner, knee-deep in water, looking down toward where the street had been. Now, there was nothing but water, churning and swirling under his flashlight. It had risen so high on the library building, the lower set of windows had disappeared entirely, and they were tall windows.

If Kate is in there, he thought grimly, striking

out from the corner with a look of fierce determination on his square-jawed face, she's in deep trouble.

"But I don't *want* to go upstairs, Sam!" Becka protested. "It's so nice down here, and we've got everything we need, and the stereo isn't portable, so we can't take it up there with us, and we won't have any music, and . . ."

Sam put up a hand, interrupting her. He knew what she was doing. Becka wasn't stupid. She had already guessed why they had to move upstairs, and she didn't want to hear it. If he said it aloud, actually *said* it, that would make it real, and she didn't want that. She was afraid.

And, he realized reluctantly, so was he.

chapter
15

Patients continued to stream into Emergency. Some had cuts and bruises from scrambling to safety as the car in which they were traveling to higher ground began to waver in the rushing waters. Others, not so lucky, were suffering from shock, broken limbs, or deep lacerations after their vehicles had been swept off the road and into a stone wall or another car. People who had waited until the last possible moment to evacuate their homes staggered in thoroughly soaked, shaken, and cold to the bone. There were two more near-drownings within seconds of each other.

Every treatment and trauma room was occupied. Susannah ran from one room to another, restocking supplies, taking information from relatives or friends, carrying hot coffee to the harried medical staff.

The moment there was another lull in activity in ER, Susannah went to the phone to see if it was working yet. The dial tone came and went.

She took a chance, dialing Abby's house, and she got through.

"No," Moira said, her voice cracking slightly. "They're not back yet."

"We should have gone for more help," Callie complained, "like I wanted. We can't get them down out of this tree by ourselves." She was clinging to the trunk of the tree as if it were a life preserver. In a way, it was. The tree was only a few yards from the riverbank, long since submerged, and the water was highest where they stood. Or tried to stand. The current was so strong, Callie was repeatedly swept off her feet, remaining where she was only because she was clutching the tree. "I can't hold on here forever, Abby," she shouted. "What are we going to do? We need help! We've been in this water for hours. It's the middle of the night already. My mother's asleep, but yours must be going crazy!"

Neither the wind nor the rain had lessened even a little bit. Callie's long hair, unrestrained in the absence of her hat, whipped around her face. She didn't dare loosen her grip on the tree to brush the hair out of her eyes.

Abby, her own hair wet, her face ruddy with windburn, hung on to the tree and shouted back, "Where would we get help? Everyone's out rescuing people from flooded houses, and from stranded cars! And we can't wait! The water's going to climb right up into this tree and pluck my sisters out if we don't do something *now*! I'm not leaving without them. Listen, you climb up onto my shoulders, okay? You're shorter than me. And lighter." Stooping to feel beneath the water with one hand, she called, "Here! I found something. There's a big, fat knot on the lower part of the tree. You can use that to push yourself up onto my shoulders. Then you can go up there and grab Carmel." Although Abby's shouts sounded steady enough, she was shaking with fear. The water was up to her waist. Carmel was only eight, and not tall like Moira and Geneva. If they did get her down out of the tree, wouldn't the water be over Carmel's head?

I'll have to carry her, Abby decided, and groaned mentally. In this current? They would probably both drown.

Abby snapped at Callie, "Well, what are you waiting for? We don't have a lot of time here, Callie. We do this kind of stuff in cheerleading all the time. It's easy."

"Yeah, well, you don't do it in the middle of a flood. And *I'm* not a cheerleader, Abby." But Callie knew there wasn't any choice. She sloshed over to grip Abby's strong, round shoulders, took a deep breath and, fumbling around with her booted foot until she found the thick knot on the tree trunk, which she used as a step, she hoisted her own slender body upward. She was

183

so water-laden, she weighed more than usual, so the maneuver that should have been a simple one for someone so lightweight and agile took far more strength than she'd expected. It took her three tries before she succeeded. When she was perched on Abby's shoulders, the boots of her heels digging painfully into Abby's flesh, Callie swayed precariously and almost fell backward into the river below her.

"Be careful!" Abby screamed.

"I can't be careful! Oh, God, this is *so* not a good idea!" But Callie steadied herself by grabbing the upper branch Carmel was lying on and clutching it with a white-knuckled grip, and reached out for Carmel's hand.

Carmel flinched. "No! I'm not moving. You'll drown me! I'm staying here until a rescue boat comes."

"No, you're *not!*" Geneva shouted from the branch above Carmel's head. "You are getting out of this tree right this minute, Carmel O'Connor! Because I can't go down until you do. You're in my way. I need that branch you're hugging. And I am *not* staying up here. Now get going!"

And although Carmel burst into tears of terror, she sat up slowly, carefully. Her sweatshirt and jeans were so wet, they clung to her skin, her short, dark hair dripped like her tears, and her eyes were wide with shock and fear. "Don't drop me, okay? Please don't drop me," she pleaded.

"What I'm going to do," Callie said as patiently as she could manage in view of her own terror, "is hand you down to your sister. She can let go of the tree with one hand and take yours. You stay right there with her now, you hear? The water is really rough, and it will pull on you, but you can't let go of Abby's hand. Promise?"

"I promise," Carmel agreed through her tears.

She weighed more than Callie had expected. A one-handed grip on a water-laden eight-year-old when perched uncertainly on someone else's shoulders high above a raging river would have been completely impossible if Callie hadn't feared for her own life. Her determination to survive allowed her to hand the terrified child down to her sister, who let go of the tree with one hand and grabbed Carmel's arm the very second it was within reach. Carmel's feet never touched the ground. The water picked her legs up and tore at them, in an earnest effort to rip her from Abby's grasp. Abby held on. So did Carmel.

But Abby didn't know how long they could hold on to each other, or how long she could bear the pain of Callie's heels digging into her shoulders, or how long Callie could remain where she was.

And Geneva was still up in the tree.

*   *   *

Three ambulances arrived at ER at once, carrying victims stranded in an office elevator when the electricity failed. Two were unconscious from lack of air, the third suffering a broken leg as a result of his heroic but disastrous attempt to climb out through the elevator's ceiling. The fourth, a pregnant woman in her third trimester, was experiencing early labor pains.

"Saw it on a movie on television," the failed hero, his words breathy and weak, told Will as the gurney rolled toward a treatment room. "This guy on TV, he saved the lives of eight people, all stranded in an elevator during a fire. Just climbed right up there and opened that little window in the ceiling, climbed out, shinnied down the cable, swung his way across to another floor, and got help. Saved all them people. Me, I couldn't even get the little door in the ceiling open. Fell right back down, clumsy as a ten-ton gorilla. Felt like a fool, I tell you. Landed on a metal cleaning cart the maintenance guy had on the elevator with him. That's how I broke my leg. How is he, anyway?"

"He'll be okay," Will answered. "He's getting oxygen now, they all are. That'll perk them right up." He steered the cart into a room where a doctor he didn't recognize and two nurses were waiting.

"What about the lady with the baby? She told

me while we were sitting there on the floor that she wasn't due for another six weeks. She going to be okay?"

"Can't tell you that. They won't bring her in here, though. They'll take her straight upstairs to OB-GYN. They'll take good care of her. Even if she does have the baby, our Neonatal Intensive Care is one of the best."

The nurses and doctor began checking the man's vital signs, which seemed to be normal. His only injury appeared to be the broken leg. And wounded pride. "Neonatal? What's that?"

"Newborn. Intensive care for preemies and babies born with problems. If that baby decides not to wait, its mother couldn't have come to a better place."

"Wish I could figure out how that guy on TV got out of that elevator," the man said, already drowsy from the medication a nurse had given him for pain.

When he had been taken upstairs to Orthopedics to have the leg set, Will went to the nurses' desk to inquire about the pregnant woman.

"She'll be fine," Nurse Thompson told him. She looked exhausted, with dark circles under her eyes. Will had never seen her looking anything but bright and cheerful. She should have stayed home, after working a double shift. "They took her upstairs. Susannah went along, for moral support. She's very good in situations like that, you know."

Will knew.

"But," Nurse Thompson continued, "I don't think they'll be keeping the woman. That baby's not going to show up tonight."

"Good. How about the other two?"

"Fine. They've already been treated and sent home. If they can get there. I'm surprised we haven't had more cases like theirs. Elevators must have stopped all over the city when the electricity went out."

"Maybe most people left work early," Will suggested. "Because of the storm." He wanted to ask if she'd heard from Kate, but she looked so tired, he couldn't do it. If she'd heard anything, she would have said so. "Aaron working on the sandbag lines?" he asked instead.

"Um-hum. Him and his father. And practically everyone else in Eastridge. They said on TV that it was bad over there." A worried frown creased her brow. "I'd go sandbag, too, if I wasn't needed here. Three of our night nurses didn't make it in." She sipped coffee from a Styrofoam cup, then added, "I wonder if our homes will be there when we return."

Will lived only two blocks from the Thompsons. "They made it through the last time. Six years ago."

Nurse Thompson nodded. "This one might be worse, though. The rain hasn't let up at all. I can't remember how long it rained that last time."

Will didn't remember, either. And he really didn't want to.

Now that Kate had the library's upstairs window wide open, she couldn't see that it had done her any good. She wasn't going to jump into that black, swirling lake beneath her window. All she seemed to have accomplished so far was soaking herself and the rose-colored carpet in the loft.

She had to do *something*. Since she couldn't go down the stairs, she would have to go *up*. Up and away from the water, which was about to swallow up the third of the six steps and was now not that far from where she stood at the top of the stairs.

Kate poked her head and upper body through the open window. She twisted slightly to glance to the side, where she noticed a thick, white drainpipe. Its lower half had disappeared beneath the water below, but the upper half edged its way up the corner of the building to the roof.

I was the first person in my sixth-grade class to climb the rope, Kate thought, studying the drainpipe. The very first.

The drainpipe was not a rope. It wasn't rough,

with fibers to cling to. It was metal and smooth and shiny, and slick with rainwater. But it was all she had.

Kate pulled back from the window, turning to look down upon the steps again. Floodwater was continuing to reach for her at a horrifyingly rapid pace.

She spun around again, facing the window, and put one leg over the low sill.

At the corner, Jeremy tried to plan the best way to get to the library without actually diving into the water and swimming. There was too much debris in the water. A kitchen chair floated by, then a cuckoo clock, and a doghouse.

He aimed his flashlight across the water toward the library. All he saw, beyond the street-sign pole and closed, dark shops, was more water, almost all the way up to the building's upper floor. No sign of life. No lights. It was just him and the rain and the wind. Jeremy raised the light, played it on the library's small, upper-story window, expecting to see nothing

Instead, he saw movement. Even with the light, he couldn't make out exactly what the movement was, or what it meant. "Kate?" he called automatically.

His voice was swallowed up by the storm. And in the next second, before he could convince himself that he really *had* seen something there in the library's upper-story window, a sudden, powerful gust of wind caught the street-sign pole, which read FIFTH STREET on one side and MARKET STREET on the other, yanked it out of the ground where it had been stationed since before Jeremy was born, and slammed it down upon Jeremy's head and back, knocking him off his feet and into the gushing torrent, face first.

"I've been trying to call the fishing lodge," Susannah told Will as they took a much-needed break. Instead of retreating to the staff lounge, they had taken up a position at the hospital's front double-glass door, where they could look out upon the storm. "I can't get through. The line isn't busy. There's just this weird sound after I dial; you know, that absence of sound you get when there's nothingness?"

"That lodge is on the South Side, right? Those lines are probably down. Ours could go out at any second, and stay out. There's a scary thought. How would anyone call us?"

"They're not calling us now, much. The phones have been quiet for the past hour. Astrid says it's because ours are probably the only working phones left in the city."

They were quiet for a few minutes. Then Will leaned against the door, facing Susannah, and said, his tone casual, "So, did you mean what you said about working in my clinic?"

"Of course I did. I wouldn't have said so if I didn't mean it."

He knew that was true. Susannah wasn't the kind of person to say things she didn't mean. Callie was, and Sam probably was, too. At least with girls. But not Susannah.

Will looked straight at her. "It'd be hard. We'd get all kinds in the kind of clinic I want. You're not really used to all kinds, Susannah. No offense, but you're not. Living up there, on that hill, so far above everybody else? Real life doesn't reach up that high, does it?"

She didn't get mad, as he'd been afraid she would. "No," she answered calmly, "real life doesn't very often intrude on Linden Hill. But," she added, her voice firm, "I work *here*, Will. And we get all kinds here, too." She lifted her chin proudly. "I think I'm pretty good at dealing with all kinds of people."

"I wasn't insulting you, Susannah," he said gently, reaching out to take her hand in his. "I just want you to know that the kind of clinic I have in mind for Eastridge won't be a piece of cake."

"I don't eat cake." Smiling up at him, Susannah curled her fingers tightly around his. "Except on my birthday. Too much cholesterol. What kind of doctor are you going to be if you don't warn people away from something so hazardous to their health?"

He laughed. "I *was* warning you away from something that could be hazardous to your health. My clinic. Is it my fault you refuse to take my warning seriously?"

They stood in the doorway, their hands linked, looking silently into each other's eyes.

chapter
16

"I have to go get one of the boats," Sam told the friend standing at his elbow, a boy named Chad Beck. They were outside, on the lodge's upper veranda. Everyone else was still inside, talking quietly, and dozing. All traces of party atmosphere had left them in the last hour when the seriousness of their situation had finally sunk in.

On the veranda, Sam used the large black flashlight to illuminate the river now surrounding them completely. It had risen to less than two feet below the spot where they stood. He was surprised by how noisy the water was. It churned and it bubbled and boiled and it smacked angrily at the doors and windows, as if it were very angry to find this large, solid obstacle in its path.

"How are you going to get to the boathouse?" Chad asked him.

"Swim." Sam's voice was grim. Swimming in that debris-laden, roiling mess wouldn't be anything like swimming in the river when it was calm, as he'd been doing all of his life. "I'll swim to the boathouse, free one of the smaller boats, and come back to get all of you."

"And how do *we* get into the boat?" Chad asked, staring anxiously down into the churning black river beneath them.

"You jump," Sam answered grimly. "And you hope your aim isn't off. Now go back inside and keep everyone busy so they don't notice I've taken a leap off this veranda."

Chad did as he'd been told.

Sam shed his sneakers, took a deep breath, and dove over the railing into the water.

The ambulance had brought in two children who had been hurled into floodwaters while hiding in a tree house from a father angry because they had neglected their chores. While they were still in their refuge, the tree had been uprooted by the powerfully angry wind and tossed into the river. Rescue crews had rescued the children, who had bravely clung to the tree throughout their long, cold, wet ride.

Their father, quietly contrite now, had arrived twenty minutes after the ambulance. Mr. Samuelson paced anxiously back and forth in the waiting room while the children were being treated for hypothermia from their stay in the cold water, abrasions from floating debris, and a broken wrist on the younger of the two boys.

They were lying on separate gurneys in the same trauma room, covered with warming blankets, their faces turned toward each other. They had stopped shivering. Their countless abrasions were being cleaned and disinfected. Susannah held the five-year-old's hand while Dr. Lincoln applied a soothing salve to the cuts, most of which were on his face, arm, and hands.

"We're really gonna get it now," the older boy told his brother. "If you thought he was mad before, wait'll you see how mad he is when we get outa here! We prob'ly won't be allowed out of the house for a *year*!"

His brother began shivering again. He was in pain because of his fractured wrist and had been given a sedative, but it hadn't taken effect yet. The wrist, still unwrapped, would be tended to upstairs in Orthopedics.

"Your father won't hit you boys, will he?" Dr. Lincoln asked calmly as she daubed antiseptic on one last cut. Susannah knew she wouldn't have asked if the boys hadn't seemed so frightened. Of course that could have been from their brush with death. "Nah." The older boy, who had said his name was Tim, burrowed deeper beneath the warming blanket. "Our dad just yells a lot, that's all. He don't believe in hittin' people smaller than him, and we're smaller than him." He heaved a deep sigh of relief. "Good thing, too."

As they left the treatment room, Dr. Lincoln

said, "You were very good with those boys in there. Calming them down, reassuring them. I saw you holding the older boy's hand when I was disinfecting his wounds. And I've seen you work with children before. You have a gift. Have you thought about a career in pediatrics?"

Susannah was surprised by the praise. Everyone in ER said that if a word of praise ever came from Dr. Lincoln's lips, it would die of shock on the way out of her mouth. She was a stern taskmaster, with very high standards.

Unsure of how to respond, Susannah said slowly, "I think . . . well, I think I might go into family practice."

"Good thinking. You're going to make a fine doctor, Grant. Keep your grades up, stay on here for experience, and apply to every school in the country. The competition is keen, you know that. You'll have to fight to get in."

That pleased Susannah more than the compliment had. She knows who I am, she thought, she knows who my father is. Everyone in the hospital knows that. But instead of taking it for granted that Samuel Grant II could use his considerable influence and equally considerable fortune to guarantee his daughter a place at Harvard or Yale, Dr. Lincoln was implying that Susannah would have to fight for that place on her own. She liked that idea, liked it very much. Besides, she already knew where she wanted to go to college. Right here in Grant. She was going to Grant University, along with Will, Kate, and Abby, no matter what kind of fit her parents threw. "I will fight for it," she promised Dr. Lincoln. "Medicine is the only field I'm interested in. So I'll do whatever I have to."

"Good. Anytime you have any questions, please feel free to come to me."

When the two had separated, Susannah hurried to the telephone again to try Abby's house.

Abby felt as if her back were going to crack in two. With Callie on her shoulders and Carmel's weight dragging on her right arm, her spine ached with a ferocious pain. "Get Geneva down!" she gasped. "Callie, hurry! I'm going to fold!"

"Can she swim?"

"Yes!"

"Geneva!" Callie shouted upward at Geneva. "Jump!"

"From *here*? It's too far! I'm up higher than Carmel was."

"Well, I *know* that, Geneva. But it's not that far to the ground anymore because the ground isn't where it used to be. In fact, it's not there at all. There's only water. The water is much higher than the ground was. So you don't have very far to jump at all. Just be prepared to start swimming the minute you land."

Turning her head to look down at Abby, Callie said, "We should all take my advice and just dive in and start swimming. Look, the water's almost up to your chest now. We can't walk in this. We've *got* to swim."

"I don't think I can," Abby said, her voice hoarse. "I think I'm too tired."

Carmel cried, "You can't be too tired, Abby. You have to take care of *me*." She started crying again. "I'm not a very good swimmer. I try, but I always sink."

"Okay, you guys, watch out below!" There was a splash to their right as Geneva hit the water and immediately began stroking away from them.

"Why didn't she do that before?" Callie complained. "And swim home? Then we wouldn't have had to go through this hell."

"Because she'd never leave Carmel!" Abby snapped. "Now, could you please get down? Before I collapse?"

Abby was never sure what, exactly, happened next. Callie tried to jump down, but something went wrong and in the next second, Callie screamed and began to topple sideways, to the right. But her feet remained firmly planted on Abby's shoulders for another moment, and that pull, plus the tug of Carmel's weight on Abby's right arm, tipped Abby sideways, too. By the time Callie's feet left her shoulders, it was too late. Abby had already lost her balance. Callie hit the water with a startled cry, and then so did Abby. Carmel, still clinging to Abby's right arm, completely disappeared beneath the surface.

Abby, splashing frantically in the deep, rushing water, trying desperately to orient herself to this newest shock, screamed Carmel's name. But the icy, viselike grip on her arm was gone.

Her little sister was gone, too.

"I hear you have magical powers with small people," Will told Susannah. She was sitting at the admissions desk and had just tried again, in vain, to call Abby's house. "Maybe we'll make pediatrics a specialty in our clinic."

She was too worried to respond. "No one answers at the O'Connor house," she said flatly, swiveling in her chair to face him.

At her failure to respond to his praise, his own face fell. And closed against her, as she'd seen it do so often before. Each time she thought they were drawing closer, breaking down the barriers between them, something happened. Sometimes it was something he said or did, sometimes she was responsible. Like now.

"I can't help it!" she cried defensively. "I know Abby would have been back here by now if she could have been. Something is really wrong. And as far as I know, Kate hasn't been heard from, either." She looked up at Will, her eyes dark with anxiety. "I haven't forgotten that sixteen people died in the last flood, Will. Sixteen!"

He relented then, his face easing again. He moved to put a comforting arm around her shoulders. "There isn't anything we can do about Abby or Kate, Susannah."

Before Susannah could respond, a call came over the PA system announcing incoming.

"This is a bad one," Dr. Izbecki called to them as he ran past, headed for the entrance. "Church bus bringing a load of teenagers back from a concert swept off the road, hit a tree, caught on fire. We've got criticals! Get everyone available down here, *now*! Call a house code, do whatever you have to, just *do* it!"

chapter
17

—⌁⌁⌁⌁⌁⌁—

Panicking, Abby began thrashing wildly against the floodwaters, screaming Carmel's name repeatedly.

"Calm down, for pete's sake!" Callie shouted, turning to swim back to Abby. "Where *is* she? Where did she go?"

Abby stopped thrashing. "I don't know! I can't see a thing!" Abby's voice caught on a sob. "Carmel doesn't swim that well, Callie. And this current . . . she's so little. . . ."

"Relax, I'll find her. You go catch up with Geneva." Without waiting for an answer, Callie took a deep breath and dove beneath the rushing water in search of Carmel.

Although Callie Matthews was the last person in the world Abby would normally have trusted to handle an emergency, she knew she had no choice now. Callie stood a much better chance of finding Carmel than Carmel's own sister, who was a competent swimmer in a nice, quiet, peaceful swimming pool but not expert enough to battle the uncontrolled fury of the Revere on its rampage.

Trusting the one person she had never expected to trust, Abby struck out after Geneva.

The victims from the bus accident had thrown ER into chaos that would have been carefully controlled, had they not been understaffed. The more seriously injured arrived by ambulance, the minor injuries by police car. All had been delivered by boat to the vehicles waiting on higher, dry ground.

Susannah and Will ran from room to room, helping wherever they could. Portable X-ray machines needed for immediate diagnosis of broken limbs and chest or head injuries flew back and forth along the busy corridors. They ran out of gauze in one treatment room, sending Susannah upstairs for more. Will temporarily took over patient charts as she ran errands, racing up the stairs because they were quicker than the elevator.

"X ray shows a pneumothorax!" Dr. Lincoln called, reaching for a chest tube. "Let's get air into this child." She was working on a patient from the bus crash whose left leg was so bloody, Susannah couldn't tell if the limb was still inside the jeans. "Chest tube!"

Susannah knew a pneumothorax was medical

terminology for a collapsed lung. Which could be deadly. Lucky for the patient that Dr. Lincoln hadn't missed it. Air would have collected around the lung, the lung would have begun pushing on the heart, shifting it so the heart couldn't fill with blood, it would quit working, and the young patient would go into cardiac arrest.

Inserting a chest tube to suck the air out of the lung so that it could re-expand was a painful procedure for the patient. But Susannah decided this particular patient, who hadn't made a sound since he'd been brought into the room, wouldn't even be aware of the pain.

At least he hadn't been burned, like some of the other patients. All of the burn victims had hastily been transferred to the Burn Unit hospital next door. They had been trapped by flames near the front door of the bus. The side door had been imploded by the collision and wouldn't open. A police officer had told the staff that someone had ripped a metal rail from one of the seats and used it as a battering ram against a bus window, creating an escape route. He was one of those who had been taken to the Burn Unit. Although no one had said so, Susannah suspected that he'd waited to escape himself until everyone else had jumped to safety, and the flames had caught up with him while he waited.

Blood and mud smeared the white tile

floors. Policemen who had accompanied incoming leaned wearily against the walls outside the rooms, drinking hot coffee, not talking. They had reports to file, and were waiting for follow-up news on the victims before going back out into the storm. They were careful to move out of the way of any wheeled or foot traffic.

If we had the burn patients, too, Susannah thought as she opened a fresh package of gauze pads, we'd be going insane. All she knew about those patients was that of the six, three were suspected to have third-degree burns, while the other four were more likely to have mostly second degree. She felt sorry for the three. If they lived, they would suffer terribly.

But she learned a moment later that they wouldn't be suffering after all. "Just got a call," a nurse named Ruby said, poking her head into treatment room three. "The severe burn patients didn't make it. Sorry." Then she disappeared as quickly as she had arrived.

"That brings the total to five," Dr. Lincoln murmured, concentrating on the stitches she was making in a deep leg laceration. "I'm keeping track."

Confused, Susannah asked, "What total?"

Lincoln lifted her head. "Fatalities. From the storm. The flood."

"There'll be more," the doctor said matter-of-factly, finishing her work with a flourish of the needle. She clipped the suture with surgical scissors. "More drownings, especially. We're just getting started, Grant. Even if we got through the night without a single drowning victim, which is as likely as me getting off work anytime soon, they'll be finding more bodies after the mud settles. They always do."

Susannah felt sick. Five people dead! She glanced up at the fat, round clock on the wall. Three twenty-six. Hours yet until dawn. And morning didn't necessarily mean an end to the storm. When Susannah cocked an ear to listen, it sounded just as loud outside as it had earlier. The wind, the rain smacking against the windows. Why did people always say things would look better in the morning? If the storm didn't end, nothing would look better. And nothing would *be* better.

"You look terrible," Astrid Thompson told her flatly when Susannah walked out to the desk. "Go into the lounge and sack out. That's an order! You aren't even supposed to be here. I chased you and Will out hours ago. If you won't lie down, you'll have to go home, and I mean that."

Susannah was too tired to argue. After a quick glance around to see where Will was, and not finding him, she went to the lounge and flopped down on the worn tweed couch.

* * *

Kate settled on the slightly peaked roof of the library, crouching on her hands and knees, rain and wind battering her mercilessly. She wondered how she had managed to climb up the slick, wet drainpipe. She couldn't believe she had made it. There had been moments when her knees, gripping the pipe tightly, had slipped, or the palms of her hands had slid an inch downward, and she had thought for sure she was going to end up in that murky mess below her.

But she hadn't. The distance from the window to the roof had been a short one, and she had been determined. So she had made it. She had no idea what to do now, but at least she had bought herself some time. It would take a while for the water seeping up the steps to climb another half-story. And that *would* happen. She didn't believe for a minute that it wouldn't. This building was lower than many of the houses in Eastridge, and she could clearly remember people there sitting on the roofs of their small homes waiting for rescue, the water nearly as high as the rooflines.

But she was safe for a moment. Wet and cold and in danger of being blown right off her perch by gusting winds that bent the trees opposite her, she was, however, still safe. Comparatively speaking.

When she thought she heard someone call her name, she was sure she was hallucinating. Her first reaction was, it's the shock of climbing up that drainpipe, knowing the whole time that I was risking my stupid life. It did something to my brain. Or my hearing. There is *no* one out there!

She shook her wet head to clear it of the illusion that someone in this dark, empty, silent world was actually speaking to her.

"Kate? Are you in there?"

Carefully, holding on tightly to the roof shingles, Kate peered over the edge. Her eyes had become accustomed now to the unbroken darkness and she was able to make out outlines and shadows. There was definitely an outline down there, something moving near the doorway. Floating? A log, a garbage can, a piece of furniture?

No, those were arms waving. That was a *person* down there?

The object shouted. "Kate! Kate, are you here?"

It *was* a person! Someone had come to get her? Who?

"Kate, answer me if you're in there!"

Kate sagged backward on her heels with relief. But she was so astonished, giddy laughter bubbled up inside her throat. Jeremy Barlow, spoiled and rich and pampered every bit as much as Callie Matthews, had braved this atrocious night to come looking for Kate Thompson?

Will's appearance on the scene wouldn't have

surprised her. He had known she intended to go to the library, and he was a close friend. Or the arrival of Sam Grant wouldn't have been such a shock. He had dropped her off here. He might have come back to offer her a safe ride home.

But Jeremy? Why wasn't he safe in his palatial home on Linden Boulevard, lying on a leather couch in his den, a fire in the fireplace she was sure the den possessed, watching television on what was surely a giant screen? What was he doing down there, swimming around in that cold, filthy water?

You *know* what he's doing down there, Kate told herself, leaning over the edge again. Hasn't he been shouting your name? He's looking for *you*, twit!

"Jeremy!" she called. "I'm up here!"

Sam was amazed at how easy it was to swim into the boathouse and untie a small motorboat. He was going in the right direction, and the current obligingly carried him swiftly to the spot where the boathouse lay underwater. He could no longer even see the roofline of the small structure. But two rowboats and a small motorboat had been yanked out of the boathouse by the current, and though still moored, were accessible to Sam. He grabbed the edge of the motorboat as he reached it.

Getting into it was no small task, given the

current and the maddening bobbing of the boat. But Sam was determined. Using his broad shoulders and considerable upper-body strength, courtesy of hours of intense tennis playing, he managed to climb into the boat. He struggled to light the lantern affixed to the front of the boat, and finally had to give up, the wind huffing out every match he lit. Then he realized it would be essential to bail before he dared pull away into open water. That took many precious minutes. When he felt it was safe to venture forth, he tried again to light the lantern and this time, succeeded. Then he wasted more valuable time fighting with the motor. It balked.

He refused to give up. The wind tugged and pulled at him angrily, the rain slapped his face, but he kept trying to bring the motor to life. He had to get those people out of the cabin.

After many tries, his perseverance was rewarded by a roar from the motor. He was on his way. He untied the boat and, using the garish yellow glow of the lantern, headed for the lodge.

When he finally reached the cabin, Chad was waiting on the upper veranda. He leaned over the railing. "Everyone's rattled!" he shouted. "The water's only got three more steps to go before it pours into the bedrooms. They thought you weren't coming back! Some of them," he added hastily.

Sam tossed him a rope. "Tie this around the

railing until we're loaded up! Then go get everyone, bring them out here! Hurry up!"

Chad did as he'd been told. When he returned, the other four were with him, their tense faces turned a sickly yellow by the light from Sam's boat.

"You'll have to jump!" Sam shouted, struggling to keep the boat as steady as possible. "Jump in, grab the rope, and follow it to the boat. I'll haul you in."

The looks on their faces told him how frightened they were at the thought of jumping into the rough water.

"You have no choice! That whole floor is going to be underwater before long! The water's only a couple of feet below you. Kind of like jumping into a pool from a diving board, right? Come on, hurry up, I can't hold the boat steady much longer!"

He saw them glance behind them, all of them, checking just one more time to see if a miracle had happened and the water behind them had stopped its mad chase.

When they turned around, it was clear that no such miracle had taken place.

Pinky Dwyer went first. She was a good swimmer, had won several awards at the country club her family and Sam's belonged to. She bobbed to the surface, grabbed the rope, and followed it to the boat, exactly as Sam had ordered. She was thin, lightweight in spite of her wet clothing, and he had no trouble hauling her into the boat.

"That was gross!" was her comment as, gasping, she fell onto the floorboards. "That water is filthy!"

Chad's girlfriend, Lisa Dane, followed Pinky. Chad and Dominic hung back, wanting to see the girls to safety before they made their try.

But Becka refused to jump.

chapter

18

The decision to dive in search of Carmel O'Connor wasn't as easy for Callie as it appeared. She hadn't realized until she toppled into the water how dangerous it had become. It was the roughness of it that kept her off-balance, the way the water surged and whirled and boiled. Like ocean surf.

Fully submerged, swimming furiously, eyes open for signs of Carmel, she had only been under a minute or two when an arm bumped against her, the fingers on its hand clawing at her frantically. Callie grabbed the arm. Hung on. Swam upward, pulling the arm along with her.

Carmel came up to the surface gasping for breath.

"Don't try to swim," Callie instructed, glancing around for Abby and Geneva. She could vaguely see shapes ahead of her struggling valiantly toward higher ground, which as far as Callie could tell, wasn't visible yet. How far were they all going to have to swim before they found a dry spot where they could rest? "If you try, and you panic, you'll drag us both down. Just hold onto me. Put your arms around my neck. I'll get you across."

Callie hoped she wasn't promising something she couldn't deliver. She had no idea how many streets the flood had swallowed up. How far was she going to have to swim in all this filth with Carmel's weight on her back?

By the time she had swum with her soggy, clinging burden across the avenue and then across three more parallel streets, all completely submerged beneath at least six feet of water, Callie had lost sight of Abby and Geneva. All she saw around her, when she gathered up enough strength to look, was darkness and the sheen of black water. Large and small objects bobbed around her, and at one point a packing crate popped up out of the water, smacking her in the cheek. It hurt.

"Didn't you see that coming?" she called over her shoulder to Carmel. "You could at least play lookout back there and give me some warning!"

Carmel's only answer was a half-sob. Her arms around Callie's neck felt like chains. The girl seemed to have gained twenty pounds, and Callie felt a sob of her own catching in her throat. She was so tired. Completely, thoroughly exhausted.

I never should have stepped one foot outside

that drugstore, Callie thought, her strokes weakening slightly. Or I should have just saved myself and left these two bratty girls to Abby. Carmel isn't *my* sister. Why isn't Abby doing this?

Because Abby couldn't have saved her, came the answer. Callie found some comfort in that. In fact, she found a *lot* of comfort in it. Everyone who knew Abby O'Connor liked her, even loved her. The same couldn't be said for Callie Matthews, could it? But who exactly *was* it out here in this wild cesspool risking her neck for Carmel O'Connor? It sure wasn't Abby.

Dry land was blocks away, several blocks past the avenue, past the center of town, past a cluster of darkened homes with water up to their second stories. It seemed likes miles. But Callie made it, with Carmel clinging to her back the entire time.

Abby and Geneva, standing on the sloping lawn of a house that sat high and dry, far above them at the top of a hill, urged Callie on with screams and shouts, from the moment the two were spotted in the water. When they were close enough, the water diminishing to no more than two feet deep, Abby ran to pick up Carmel, and waited to help Callie to her feet.

Together, the four climbed to the top of the hill. If there had been any signs of life in the house, they would have knocked until someone answered. But the house was clearly deserted, and there were no cars in the driveway or, when Abby checked through the window, in the garage. Empty.

She would have broken in and used the telephone to call her mother, but Callie pointed to a tree down in the side yard amidst a tangle of wires. "Wouldn't do you any good," she said. "Those look like telephone lines."

Too tired to trek over to the house next door, which looked equally deserted, they all climbed up on the front porch and collapsed under the shelter of the porch roof. Huddled together, they were asleep in minutes.

They were awakened some time later by the unmistakable sound of a boat's motor approaching from the north.

Help was on the way.

It was Will who awakened Susannah. He knelt beside her, touching her hand and speaking her name quietly. She stirred and rolled over on the tweed couch, opening her eyes quickly, as she always did upon awakening. "What's wrong?"

He knelt beside her. "A rescue crew just came in from the South Side. They said your dad's fishing lodge was underwater. Only the roof is showing. I thought you should know."

Susannah sat up, rubbing her eyes, knowing her mascara had probably streaked, but not caring. "Sam?"

"I don't know. They picked up an elderly couple, but there wasn't any sign of Sam. They're going to take another run down that way, but they said it's getting pretty dangerous out there."

"Did you rest at all?" Susannah asked Will. Her eyes felt gritty, she knew her hair had to be matted from lying down, and what little makeup she'd been wearing had long ago faded from existence.

"Yeah, I did." He waved toward a worn, flowered chair opposite her couch. "I sacked out there." He grinned. "You look good asleep. Not everyone can say that. Some people, their faces look like putty when they're sleeping. Nothing stays where it's supposed to. I've seen lots of patients who look like that when they're asleep. But not you. Everything stays in its own perfect place."

Too flustered to accept the compliment, Susannah failed to acknowledge it. Instead, she asked as she stood up, "Has anyone heard from Kate? Or Abby?"

"I don't know." His voice had turned cool. "I told you, I was sleeping."

She knew she should have at least said thank you. What he had said to her was nice, not the kind of thing a girl heard every day. And she'd ignored it. But he'd picked a terrible time to say it. She wasn't in the mood.

"I did hear, though," he added in a more normal tone of voice, "that we had two more fatalities. Before I came in here. Two drownings, at a low-water crossing. A man and his wife in a car. Their kid survived. Ten-year-old boy. He was in the backseat of the car, and got out through a window. The parents were trapped, and the car was swept away."

"That makes six," Susannah said, horror in her eyes. "Six dead. And it's not even morning yet."

Will glanced down at his watch. "Yeah, it is. It's after five. Twenty after. Think any of the day shift'll make it in at seven?"

"I don't know. I can't believe I slept that long. Is it still raining?"

Together, they went to the window to check. It was still raining. Heavily.

Becka never did jump from the veranda. Chad, acknowledging a signal from Sam via eye contact, reached out finally and gave the terrified girl a shove. She tumbled over the railing and into the water. Chad was right behind her. The minute he came back up to the surface, he grabbed the collar of her shirt and hauled her over to the boat.

"You'll forgive us someday," Sam told her as he pulled her in.

When they were all in the boat, he cut the rope with his penknife and turned the boat around to head upriver, toward the city. It would have been easier traveling in the opposite direction, with the current, but he was afraid that if they got too far away from the city, hope of rescue would lessen. His plan was to head straight for the arched stone bridge in the center of the city. Unless he was mistaken, that bridge should be level with the water right about now. He could drive the boat right up to it and they could all step out onto the safety of the bridge. Even if the bridge happened to be completely underwater by now, they'd still have a better chance of running into a bigger rescue boat if they went toward the city instead of away from it.

"Hang on, everyone!" he shouted. "This is going to be the ride of your life! And keep your eyes out for junk in the water, okay? Yell when you see anything larger than a doorknob."

Sam wished, as he spurred the boat into action, that he'd been able to locate life jackets in the boathouse. He hadn't been able to see well enough, and there hadn't been time to hunt.

No one in the boat was wearing one.

"I'm surprised to see you down here," a nurse said to Sid Costello, who was sitting in the doorway of Rehab's makeshift shelter, a pile of white towels in his lap. "Surprised in a nice way, of course. You're all dressed. You look nice. Who helped you? I didn't even know you were gone.

219

I'm curious about what got you out of that mood you were in."

"Tiger helped me." Tiger was a big, friendly orderly Sid knew and trusted. "He got me out of bed and helped me dress."

"You didn't answer my question." The noise level in the room had increased. The nurse had to raise her voice, even though she was still standing beside his chair. "It's really great to see you rejoining the real world, even helping out, but what got you going?" She smiled. "I'll bet it was that girl. The one you wanted me to call. I tried, but I couldn't get through. Sorry." She glanced around the room. "Is she here?"

"No. She isn't." Disappointment hardened Sid's voice. "And I came down because I was sick of that stupid room, that's all. It didn't have anything to do with her."

"Um-hum. Well, if you're tired, I can take you back upstairs now."

"I'm not tired. I'll stay."

"Well, okay then. Just keep doing your thing, handing out those towels, okay? Your friend will show up sooner or later. The electricity is still on in north and west Grant, so the hospital put out a call on radio for volunteers to come and help out here."

Sid brightened. She'll come, he thought. Abby will come if she hears.

Sid wheeled his chair around and set it in motion toward the door to greet new arrivals with clean, still-warm towels.

Jeremy was not that far below Kate. The water, bringing Jeremy with it, had risen almost to the second-story window.

"Jeremy," she called down from her perch at the edge of the roof, "what are you going here?"

"Looking for you. I've been looking for you all night long. I would have been here sooner, but I was attacked by a street sign. Probably would have drowned if the water wasn't so damn cold. It revived me, fast!" He was clinging to the windowsill, his legs floating out behind him. She thought his teeth were chattering, but she couldn't be sure. "How did you get up there?"

"I came by way of the drainpipe. Just checking on the shingles up here," she added lightly, "seeing if they'll hold up under the storm. I repeat, what are you doing here?"

"I came to get you."

That struck Kate as almost funny. Get her? And do what? How was he going to get her to dry land, if there was such a thing left somewhere in the city? "Jeremy, I can't swim."

She could tell by the sudden silence that he was shocked. In Jeremy's world, everyone swam and skied and played tennis almost from the moment they were born. "*You can't swim?*" He said it in the same tone of voice he might have used to say, "You can't read?"

"No, Jeremy," Kate answered sarcastically, "I just never did make it to the country club for those lessons."

"You can't swim," he repeated. After a moment, he said, "Well, okay. I'll just go get us a boat. I know where they are."

"A boat? Jeremy, there isn't time! The water's going to be up to the roof soon."

"I'll be right back, I promise. Don't go away."

chapter
19

—⎍⌵⍀⎍⌵⍀⎍⌵⍀⎍⌵⍀⎍⌵⍀⎍—

Abby and her sisters and Callie were taken by boat to ambulances waiting on dry ground, and then to ER, in spite of Abby's protestations that they were all fine and just wanted to go home.

"Speak for yourself!" Callie snapped as they were helped up into an ambulance. The idea of being fussed over at ER appealed to her. Her father wouldn't have left the hospital that night during an emergency situation. He'd still be there. They'd call upstairs and tell him his daughter had been brought in, and he'd come rushing down to ER. Maybe they'd even tell him she saved someone's life. Because she *had,* hadn't she? And she wanted every single bit of credit that was due her. Otherwise, what was the point?

Abby hadn't even said thank you yet.

"Thank you, Callie," Abby said. She was sitting on one of two ambulance cots with her arms around both her sisters. All three were shivering, and Carmel had been seized by a coughing spasm. One of the paramedics began checking her for signs of acidosis, common among near-drowning victims, but quickly realized that Carmel hadn't come that close to drowning.

Thanks to *me*, Callie, lying on the second cot, thought. To Abby, she said, "You're welcome. But you owe me big time." Although she wasn't feeling sick, just tired, she didn't argue when the second paramedic wrapped a blood pressure cuff around her upper arm. If she looked too healthy, they'd just send her home. They wouldn't even bother calling her father. That wasn't going to happen if she could help it.

"How are things at Med Center?" Abby asked the paramedics. "Awful, I'll bet. Any fatalities from the flood?"

She was shocked by the answer. Six. *Six?*

"And that doesn't count actual flood victims," he added. "We don't know about those yet. There are still people missing. Actually," he told Abby, "your mother reported *you* missing. You and your sisters."

"But not me?" Callie asked, disappointed. She knew why, though. Her mother, who never stayed awake late because of her illness, would have tired of waiting for Callie to return from the drugstore and fallen asleep. And her father, of course, thought she was safely at home in West Grant with her mother.

Still, it would have been nice to know that she couldn't stay out all night in atrocious weather without *someone* going ballistic.

"You all live in West Grant?" the paramedic asked. He hadn't inquired about what they'd been doing near the riverbank. Abby was grateful. She nodded in answer to his question. "Well," he continued, "if you can't get through to your house by phone when we get to ER, and you all check out okay, we'll see that you get home. Your parents must be frantic about now."

But only Geneva and Carmel went home. Abby was able to get through to the house, quickly explaining that they were all fine, that she was sending her sisters home, but she would be staying. She was needed at Rehab. Her mother was too relieved to be angry. That would come later, Abby knew, when things had returned to normal.

Callie didn't go home, either. She felt fine, although she let the nurses and doctors in ER fuss over her. Her father did come downstairs to the treatment room where she lay on a table. But once he had ascertained that she was in no danger, all he wanted to know was what on earth she had been doing out on a night like last night? When he was positive she was okay, he retreated back to his office complex on the tenth floor.

Dr. Lincoln saw the look on Callie's face and said sympathetically, "He's really got his hands full this morning, Callie. It's been a horrible night."

"Yeah, hasn't it?" Callie slid off the table. Her

moment in the spotlight hadn't lasted very long. Still, she could see that this place was where the action was. Why go home and be bored to tears when the excitement was right here? Anyway, her mother would sleep until ten or so, and it was only seven-thirty now. The visiting nurse lived in West Grant and shouldn't have any problem getting to the house. So why go home?

But since Callie could imagine the look on Abby's face if she said she was staying for the excitement, what she said instead was, "I want to help at Rehab."

"You *do*?"

Did she have to look *that* surprised? Hadn't Callie just saved her sister's life? O'Connor was an ungrateful wretch! "Yeah, I *do*," Callie replied acidly. A really good-looking young doctor passed them in the hallway. Callie flashed him a brilliant smile. Staying was an even better idea than she'd thought at first. "Is that so weird, O'Connor?"

Abby, her cheeks windburned, her wet hair curling around her face, said hastily, "Oh, no, I didn't mean that, Callie. I just thought you'd be really tired, that's all." She had changed out of her wet clothes into a borrowed nurse's aide's uniform and a pair of white shoes. "Of course you can help. They need all the help they can get."

"Are there any more of those dry uniforms

around anywhere?" Callie asked sharply. "Maybe in red? It's my best color."

Rolling her eyes, Abby pointed her in the right direction, and Callie hurried off.

"You didn't see Kate or Jeremy out there anywhere when you were wandering around in the rain, did you?" Susannah asked Abby anxiously. Susannah had never been as relieved in her life as she had been when that ambulance pulled up and Abby stepped out. Wasn't *carried out on a stretcher,* but stepped out. She was soaked and pale and shivering, but she was okay. And she had found her sisters, who were also okay.

Abby shook her head. "No. Why?"

Susannah explained.

"Kate couldn't possibly still be at the library," Abby said. "That whole area is flooded now."

Kate was lying prone on the edge of the roof. She was so thoroughly drenched, water ran from her ears. Dawn had come quickly, brightening the sky only slightly. She could see now, and what she saw was that Jeremy had not returned with the promised boat. Morning had brought no other activity on the street below her. The houses still looked deserted, the shops along Market Street were still closed, and there was no traffic, boat or otherwise, on the flooded streets. She could hear distant sounds . . . voices shouting . . . a boat's motor, she thought, though she couldn't be sure . . . the faraway wail of an ambulance. But the usual morning sounds of cars starting, buses chugging past her house, the whistle of a train, radios blasting through open windows in Eastridge, people calling to each other as they carried the trash to the curb . . . those sounds were absent. Instead, her vigil on the library's roof was accompanied only by the dull roar of the harsh, steady wind, the slapping of the rain on the shingles, and the hungry lapping of the water now no more than a foot and a half below where she lay on her stomach.

She raised her head, looked around her, and saw nothing moving but the tree branches over her head. If I have to, she vowed, I will climb that tree, clear up to the top branches. But I don't *want* to.

"Jeremy!" she shouted, "where *are* you?"

The arrival of morning, gray and dismal as it was, hadn't done Sam much good. Visibility had increased only slightly, and it seemed to him the wind had picked up. His back and shoulders ached, his eyes burned from constantly battling a fierce wind and the steady spray of dirty water hitting his face, and he'd never been so tired in his life. Twice, the current had yanked the boat into a cove, not shallow enough for anyone to jump out and swim to safety, but so debris-laden, he'd had to fight to get the boat back out into the swollen river again.

The five others were crouched in the bottom of the boat, bailing steadily with bait cans. Becka looked wet and tired, but she never once stopped slopping the water out of the boat. All of them looked pale and drained.

When Sam spotted what was still visible of the arched stone bridge spanning the Revere in the center of the city, he thought at first he was hallucinating. Even though it never should have taken them all night to reach the bridge, even though he'd expected to arrive at this point hours ago, when he did see his goal approaching, he still couldn't believe it.

"There it is!" he shouted, "there's the bridge! We made it!"

His exhausted passengers swiveled their heads to look.

They were still too far away to see exactly how much of the bridge, if any, was still dry. Even if only the stone railing was clear, he could steady the boat against one of the pillars while everyone climbed on to the railing and crawled or walked along it to Massachusetts Avenue on the other side. If the avenue was underwater, they'd have to swim it until they reached high ground. But at least they were back in civilization again.

It hit Sam, then, how alone he had felt trying

to steer this boat back to the city. True, everyone had bailed, everyone had shouted their support, no one had complained. But they were his guests, they had come into the South Side at his urging, and he alone was completely responsible for getting them back to safety.

He had done that. Well, almost.

Keeping his eyes fixed on the curve of the bridge, Sam steered around the flotsam and jetsam floating in the water.

It was Chad who jumped to his feet. Later, he would admit that he knew better. Growing up, he'd spent long hours on the family boat, much bigger than this little craft, on the river. He knew about boats. He even knew about floods, and dangerous water. His excuse was, he'd become so excited at the thought of rescue when Sam shouted that they'd reached the bridge, that he'd forgotten everything he'd learned about boats and water. And he jumped to his feet.

In spite of the steady, arduous bailing, the bottom still held an ample supply of rainwater. When Chad stood up, the boat rocked. All of the water in the bottom immediately slopped to his side of the boat, tilting it precariously.

But it still wouldn't have tipped over if Becka, and then the other two girls in the boat, hadn't become caught up in Chad's enthusiasm and followed his example. Because they had both been sitting on Chad's side of the boat, their sudden motions as they jumped up, combined with the slop of the water that hadn't yet been bailed, tilted the boat so far over on its side that the Revere, accepting the invitation, rushed right in.

"Sit down!" Sam screamed, knowing it was too late.

It was.

The boat went over quietly, spilling all six occupants into the turbulent, muddy water.

chapter
20

Samuel Grant II, dapper as always in a black trenchcoat, a black hat over his white hair, strode into ER as if he owned the planet. Almost, Susannah thought. His ancestors had founded Med Center, the University, the refinery, and Grant Pharmaceuticals. As far back as Susannah could remember, her father had walked with that distinctive, authoritative stride. She couldn't imagine him slowing his pace long enough to smell any roses along the way.

"Where is your brother?" he demanded when he reached Susannah and Will. They had just come from trauma room three, where Jeremy's father, head of Cardiology, had, against all medical odds, revived a seventeen-year-old who had been found lying under a wrecked pick-up truck, her face submerged in six inches of thick, gooey mud. She had nearly suffocated. She was in bad shape when they brought her in.

Susannah knew the girl, she realized, when the face had been hastily wiped clean for resuscitation efforts. She was also a student at The Hannah Rose Grant Day School. Cheerful and friendly and very smart. Treasurer of their class. Her name was Daphne Underwood, and Susannah was sickened by how close she had come to a horrible death.

Technically, Daphne *was* dead when they rushed her into ER. The paramedics had had no luck reestablishing a heartbeat. She had no pulse, and her lips were blue under the thick coating of mud.

But Dr. Barlow, as always, had refused to give up. He had eventually cracked the girl's chest open and massaged the heart manually until it began beating again, something Dr. Izbecki, Susannah knew, didn't approve of. Said it seldom did any lasting good.

And maybe it wouldn't this time, either. Maybe Daphne wouldn't make it. Her chances weren't very good. But when Susannah and Will left the trauma room, Daphne was alive, thanks to Dr. Barlow.

Seeing Daphne lying on that table, her mouth and nose and eyes covered with thick, black, gooey mud, had shaken Susannah to the core.

Now, standing in the lobby as her father waited for an answer to his question about Sam, Susannah was still too shaken to think of an answer. In the past, she had sometimes fibbed for her twin. If he knew ahead of time that he was going to be coming home from a party later than he was supposed to, he occasionally asked her to cover for him; to make something up, and sometimes she did. Their father wasn't as strict with Sam as he was with his daughter, which, although unfair, Susannah had accepted, but he did have rules for Sam. Since she knew Sam wasn't really up to anything horrible, she had fibbed for him.

But not tonight. She was too tired to fib. And besides, she was worried sick about her brother. Her father could find out faster than she could exactly where Sam was and what he was doing, and if he was all right. Her father, unquestionably the most powerful man in town, had ways of finding out such things.

Susannah leaned against the reception desk and told the truth. "Sam's at the fishing lodge. At least, he was. He was holding a party down there."

Although Samuel Grant's hair was snow-white, his face was young, evenly tanned, and unlined. It tightened now with anger. "The lodge? He's on the South Side?"

"Maybe he left," Susannah said hastily, "when he saw how bad the weather was getting." But they both knew that if he had left while it was safe to leave, he would have been home by morning. Sam stayed out late partying, but he had never stayed out all night.

"Then why isn't he home where he belongs?"

Samuel Grant removed his hat to shake it dry, then put it back on his head, saying sharply, "That boy ought to have his head examined! If I find him, I'm taking him straight to the Psych building!" Then he turned on his heel and left the hospital.

"Whew!" Will said in awe. "Sam's really in for it, isn't he?"

Susannah made a rude sound. "Are you kidding? My dad'll be so glad to see him when he finds him, he'll probably buy him something new. Won't be a car. The van's too new. Maybe new skiing equipment, or a computer. Something."

"He sounded mad."

Shrugging, Susannah said, "Well, he is. Right now. But he and Sam are tight." She wasn't aware of the note of wistfulness in her voice, nor did she notice Will's eyes on her in sympathy. "Dad will forgive Sam anything. He likes to think of the two of them as pals. Anyway, he always sounds madder when he's worried, and he's worried now. I can tell. So am I. That paramedic who came in with Daphne said the South Side is completely underwater now. Everyone's been evacuated. But the lodge is so isolated. There isn't a neighbor around for miles. Unless Sam had the portable radio on, he wouldn't have known about the evacuation order. And I'd bet he had his stereo on instead."

"He can see water rising, can't he?"

"Not if he's too busy partying to pay attention."

Will reached out to brush a strand of fair hair away from Susannah's cheek. "He'll be okay."

"That's what we said about Kate, and we still haven't heard from her," she answered, tears in her eyes. "I'm going to ask her mother straight out if she's heard from Kate. I don't know what else to do."

"No," Astrid Thompson answered when Susannah posed the question. "I haven't heard anything." She was filing medical charts. Susannah noticed that her hands were shaking slightly, although her voice was composed. "I tried to call the librarian at home, but his phone is out. Kate's not on any of the rescue crews' lists, and all I know is, she hasn't been brought in here injured. That's a good sign, don't you think?"

"Yes," Susannah told Kate's mother in a firm voice, "I think that's a very good sign. I'm sure Kate is fine." She was, of course, lying.

When Kate awoke, the first thing she was aware of was her astonishment that she'd actually fallen asleep on the roof. The second thing she became aware of was that the rain had stopped. It was still drizzling faintly, a fine mist, but to the north, the sky was slowly beginning to turn a paler shade of gray mixed with a watery, translucent blue.

She sat up. Her muscles, stiff from lying on the rough shingles, groaned a protest. The water had risen to less than a foot below the roofline. She could have washed her hands in it without stretching if she'd wanted to. She didn't. It was filthy, a brackish brown, littered with debris.

But it was no longer rising. And it had quieted. The bubbling and boiling had stopped. The water lay still now, an ugly, foul-smelling, brown blanket spread over much of the city of Grant.

The flooded street showed no signs of life. And Kate heard no sound but the chirping of a few birds. Of course they're chirping, she thought sourly, brushing a loose strand of dark hair back from her forehead, because they can fly *over* all this mess. I never wanted wings before, but they'd come in handy right now.

Jeremy hadn't returned with the promised boat.

Not that she'd really expected him to. Jeremy was decent enough, in spite of his moodiness, but he wasn't Will. Will would have returned immediately with a boat. Sam probably would have, too. Jeremy's problem was that he let himself be intimidated by his father. Impossible to measure up to such perfection. Of course, everyone else who knew Dr. Barlow found him intimidating, too, so she didn't really blame Jeremy. He should have gone to San Francisco with his mother, made a fresh start with people who didn't even know Dr. Barlow. She knew why he hadn't gone. Because he thought his mother wasn't going to have any money. Jeremy liked having money. Personally, Kate thought, Jeremy would be better off with less money and more independence. He'd never have either living with his father.

Dr. Barlow would have been back with a boat by now, too. Maybe two boats. With caviar and champagne on board.

Kate sat back on her heels. Her sweatshirt and jeans were cold and clammy, her hair felt stiff and matted, and the morning was much colder than yesterday, when she'd dressed. She could have used a sweater or two. She was freezing.

"Well, if I'd known I was going to end up on a roof," she murmured crankily, trying in vain to smooth her hair again, "in the middle of a flood on a freezing cold morning, I'd have dressed for it!"

She was so lost in discomfort and cold that she almost didn't hear the slapping of oars in the water as the boat approached. When she did hear it, she leaned forward, close to the roof's edge, and let her eyes survey the quiet, brown lake spread out below her.

And there he was, rowing toward her with great effort through the debris-laden water, steering cautiously around trees poking up out of the water, steering around buildings. "Kate?" he called as he got closer. She saw him craning his neck, trying to catch a glimpse of her. "Kate, are you still up there?"

His blonde hair was plastered against his head, his sweatshirt was filthy, his face smeared with mud. He looked exhausted.

But Jeremy Barlow had probably never looked as good to anyone in his life as he did at that moment to Kate Thompson.

"Yes!" she shouted, rising to her knees. "Yes, I'm still here! Where else would I be?"

Because Abby was wearing a nurse's aide's uniform, Sid didn't notice her when she entered Rehab. After her sisters had been thoroughly checked out by Dr. Lincoln, they had been dried off, warmed up, and given the okay to go home. Immediately afterward, Abby had left ER to hurry through the passageway to Rehab. Callie was at her side, complaining that white made her look "washed out."

Callie never did help. She spotted a friend when they entered the building, and hurried off, eager to start spreading the news that she was a heroine.

Abby might have protested if she hadn't been

completely caught off-guard by the sight of Sid, sitting in his chair at the entrance to The Ballroom. He was wearing a sweater instead of his usual plaid bathrobe. He looked, Abby thought, very handsome. There was a pile of white towels in his lap, a piece of paper and a pen in his hands. Taking names, Abby decided. Sid was actually handing out towels and taking names instead of brooding up in his room. She could hardly believe it.

Since Sid hadn't noticed her, she stood in the doorway, watching him. He looked so different. It wasn't just that he was dressed in street clothes, the first time she'd seen him out of his robe since she'd known him. It was more than that. He seemed to be sitting up straighter than usual. And if she hadn't known better, she would have sworn he had just smiled at a little boy clutching a catcher's mitt who'd stopped to talk to Sid on the way in.

Nah. Not Sid. Couldn't be. Wasn't smiling against his religion or something?

Then he glanced over his shoulder and saw her standing in the doorway. He didn't recognize her at first, because of the unform. He looked away, then did a great double take, jerking his head around a second time to take another look. And then he *did* smile, a big, genuine, man-am-I-glad-to-see-you smile that sent a delicious shiver down Abby's spine.

Well, surprise, surprise! she thought as she left the doorway to move toward him. And isn't *he* gorgeous when he smiles! When Abby had first met Sid Costello, she had fantasized that *she* would be the one to change his attitude, give him a reason to live, help him see that he had a future, after all. In her fantasies, she had been the one to show him that he could still be useful.

Now, there he was, fully dressed in street clothes, handing out towels, functioning perfectly fine. And she hadn't even *been* here. Couldn't take any of the credit.

Shame on you, Abby O'Connor! she scolded mentally. You should be thrilled that he's not hiding up in his room. Don't be so selfish.

She *was* thrilled. Besides, she hadn't been getting anywhere with him, anyway. Must have been her bedside manner. She'd have to work on that.

He was still smiling. It didn't bother her that when she reached his chair, the smile disappeared and he said in the same rude tone of voice she was used to, "Well, where the hell have *you* been?"

Instead of answering, she bent down and planted a firm, earnest, no-nonsense kiss on his mouth. She wasn't sure why. He'd never acted the least bit interested in kissing her. But, the thing was, *she* felt like kissing *him*. So she did.

And if she was going to kiss him, she was going to do it right. The kiss lasted at least a minute, and during that minute, she could feel him responding, first with surprise, then with what was unquestionably enthusiasm.

When the kiss ended and Abby straightened up, smiling, an equally enthusiastic round of applause sounded from The Ballroom. Everyone in the crowded room had been watching, and all were smiling.

"What'd you do that for?" Sid asked, a healthy flush in his strong-boned cheeks.

"I just wanted to cheer them all up," Abby answered lightly, smiling as she reached down to take half a dozen folded towels from his lap. "They've had a really bad night." Her eyes met Sid's. "You don't mind that I used you to entertain them, do you?"

He didn't look away, not this time. "No," he said, his eyes staying on hers. "I don't mind at all. I'm here to help."

Abby laughed.

chapter
21

Sam's first thought as he hit the turbulent water was Becka. She didn't swim well. She had to be tired from the long night behind them. She'd been soaked through and shivering with cold even before she hit the water. She wouldn't have much strength to fight the current.

When he spit himself out onto the surface, he glanced around anxiously for some sign of her. He found the other four right away. They were clinging to the overturned boat. But he saw no sign of Becka.

"Where is she?" he shouted, and Chad waved toward the bridge.

Sam saw her then. She was struggling, fighting more valiantly than he'd have expected, given her exhaustion. She hated deep water, he knew that. Swam only in pools, and never in the deep part where she couldn't touch bottom.

No way was he going to let Becka die. He was the one who had talked her into heading for the South Side. She hadn't complained, and she'd kept bailing when he knew her shoulders had to be on fire from the constant motion. She was going to come out of this okay. He'd make sure of it.

Becka's eyes were wild with fear when he reached her. When he clutched her around the waist, she panicked. Her arms flew out and fastened around his throat in a grip so tight, sharp knives of pain scissored their way up into his scalp.

"Let go!" he shouted. "Becka, let go! Let me do it! Let yourself go limp. I'll get us both back to the boat. We can hold on there until a rescue boat comes by." He sounded far more optimistic than he felt. Hanging on to her was hard enough. How was he going to hold on to Becka *and* the boat?

Had anyone else come after Becka, she might have continued to fight. But she trusted Sam to save her. He could see it in her eyes, and then she stopped struggling and let herself go limp.

His chest aching, Sam swam with her back to the boat.

The six of them hung there like barnacles, bounced around and battered by the churning water, waiting for rescue.

It stopped raining.

"Took you long enough," Kate grumbled, climbing off the roof and into the boat Jeremy had pulled alongside the library. "Where'd you go to commandeer this fine craft, Barlow?"

Gray-faced with fatigue, he answered hoarsely, "Sorry. Actually, I was only gone ninety minutes. Took me forever to get to where the boats were. Too much junk floating in the water." There were countless scratches on his face, some of which were deep and bleeding in thin rivulets. When Kate was seated, she reached out to gently swipe at a cut on his chin. Jeremy winced. "Got sideswiped by a saw," he explained as he began rowing again, this time north, toward drier streets. "Good thing it wasn't a power saw."

"Wouldn't have mattered," Kate said, swaying slightly on her seat as the boat turned. "Electricity's off."

Jeremy laughed. "Anyway, when I finally got to the boats, they were all gone. I had to wait for one to come back. The guy didn't want me to take it, but I told him there was a pregnant lady in one of the houses about to give birth, so he gave in."

"I'm supposed to be a pregnant lady?"

"Yeah, well, it worked, didn't it?" He steered around the top section of an old oak tree. "It's a mess out there, Kate. Out *here*. I've never seen so much water in my life. And if Med Center wasn't up on that knoll, it'd be flooded, too."

They sat in somber silence as Jeremy rowed up

the flooded street. "It's so deserted," he commented then. "Nobody's out, except the rescue boats and police. They have to collect people in the boats and then take them to the ambulances waiting in the north and west parts of the city. Takes too much time, but there's no other way."

"Is Sam all right?" Kate asked after another few minutes of silence. The only sound they heard was the swishing of the oars and an occasional clink as one of them collided with a floating object. "He was on the South Side, right?"

"I haven't heard. Are *you* okay? You look . . . well, kind of out of it."

Kate laughed weakly. "Out of it? I wish I *had* been out of it. Out of the storm, out of the library, out of the flood. Safe at Med Center, that's where I wish I'd been." Then, more seriously, she added, "I think I might be suffering from mild exposure. I can't stop shivering, but I feel hot inside. Might have a fever. We'd better go to Med Center, have Dr. Izbecki or Dr. Lincoln check me out. I can't afford to get sick. Anyway, I can't go home. I don't even know if my house is still there. Was my mother still on duty the last time you were in ER?"

Jeremy nodded. "Yeah. She looked beat, but she was still there. And I think the rest of your family's out on the sandbag lines."

"Yeah, they would be." Concern in her voice, Kate said, "I think you should get checked out, too, Jeremy. You look as bad as I do. And you need dry clothes, like right away. You can borrow a doctor's surgical greens." Kate reached out again to gently wipe a smear of blood from a cut on his cheek. He had risked his own life to save hers. He could have just told the rescue crew where she was, but he hadn't. He had come for her himself.

Spurred on by her remarks, Jeremy got them to the waiting ambulances without smashing into a street sign or overturning the boat.

When Susannah heard the announcement over the PA system of six incoming rescued from floodwaters near the bridge, she knew Sam would be one of the six. She had no idea why she believed this. Sam hadn't *been* near the bridge. He'd been on the South Side. And he'd probably had far more than only five people with him. Still, the feeling that he would be one of the six was so strong, she ran to the doctor's locker room and borrowed a set of whites from one of the interns, hoping with all her heart that her twin would need nothing more than dry clothing. No stitches, no casts, no EKG to find out if his heart was functioning, no oxygen, no X rays. He'd be wet, as anyone pulled from the river would be, but that . . . was . . . *all*!

Her prayers were answered. He wasn't even lying on a gurney when he was brought in, but running along beside Becka's, who looked very much as if she hadn't been as lucky as Sam. He and his other four friends, although thoroughly drenched as anyone pulled from the river would have been, seemed to be intact.

"She's breathing, but not very well!" he gasped when he saw Susannah. "She was fine at first when I got her back to the boat, but I think something in the water cracked her on the head just before the rescue boat arrived. She made a sound, and then she went limp. She went under and I had to dive for her. I think she's swallowed a lot of water."

Becka also had a nasty cut on her forehead. The blood had been washed away, but the laceration was jagged, the flesh around it swollen and purplish. "What did she hit her head on?" one of the paramedics asked as the gurney reached trauma room five and entered.

"I didn't know she hit it on anything. Something must have slammed into her while we were hanging on to the boat. There's so much junk in the water." Sam looked at Susannah. "Is it serious?"

She shook her head. Becka wasn't completely limp. In fact, she was beginning to stir restlessly on the gurney. That was a good sign. "I don't know. Maybe not." She knew how Sam would feel if Becka didn't make it. He'd blame himself. And how would he ever tell Becka's mother?

Dr. Izbecki and Dr. Lincoln were each taking a much-needed nap. The doctor on duty was one Susannah didn't know well. He was young, energetic in spite of the fact that he'd been up all night, and wasted no time administering care to the injured girl. His decision was that she didn't need a tube in her lungs, and ordered X rays just to be sure.

Becka began coughing, then, almost choking, and vomited up volumes of brown liquid.

Sam looked alarmed, but Susannah said quickly, "No, that's good. She needs to get rid of it. It's okay, Sam."

"I should call her mother," he said morosely. "God, I dread it!"

"I'll do it," Susannah offered, somewhat reluctantly. "I'll try to call her mother." It was a call she didn't want to make, either. She could have waited and let a doctor or nurse do it, but that didn't seem fair. And she had no idea how long they would be working on Becka. "Were the phones out at the cabin?" she asked Sam.

He nodded.

That meant Becka's mother hadn't heard from her all night. The woman had to be crazy with fear. "I'll call her," Susannah said, and hurried from the room.

Mrs. Downing's phone was still in operation, and she handled Susannah's call well. "I'll be right there," she said, and hung up.

Susannah dreaded returning to the trauma room. What if Becka hadn't responded?

I'll know the minute I walk in there by the look on Sam's face, she thought, her steps slower than usual as she returned to the crowded cubicle. Becka was hidden behind a row of white uniforms, but Sam breathed, "She's going to be okay," as Susannah reached his side. "She's breathing better."

She was not only breathing better, she was far more responsive now than little Louie Murphy, who had been transferred to Women's and Children's Hospital in the complex and was still in a coma. Every cough from Becka lifted Susannah's spirits further.

The doctor, however, was concerned about the head wound, and sent the shaken, shivering girl up to X Ray for a CAT scan, calling a neurosurgeon to meet the gurney upstairs.

"You're sure she's going to be okay?" Sam asked one of the nurses as the gurney disappeared.

"Looks that way." The nurse fixed a critical eye on him. "This hospital wouldn't be nearly as crowded tonight," she told him tartly, "if people like you had stayed home where you belonged."

Sam raised his hands in mock self-defense. "You won't get any argument from me," he said. "Thanks for helping Becka."

The nurse thawed a little then, adding, "She

was lucky, that's all," as she left the room.

"Here, put these on," Susannah said, handing Sam the dry whites. "And you'd better call Mom and Dad. He was here looking for you. He was *not* happy when he found out where you were."

Sam groaned. "You *told* him?"

Now that the crisis is over, Susannah realized, and he has saved Becka's life, he's back to worrying about his own neck. Well, that's Sam. "Yes, I told him. And I hope he hangs you from a beam in the family room. I've been worried sick about you all night long. You and Abby and Kate."

"Kate? What about Kate? She was at the library."

"It flooded. Jeremy went looking for her, but . . ." Before Susannah could finish the sentence, Will stuck his head in the doorway and said, "Susannah! Kate and Jeremy are here!"

Susannah turned and ran.

Kate was a sorry sight, but she looked beautiful to Susannah, who ran and hugged her. "Where on earth have you been?" She ran to the cabinet to grab a blanket, running back to wrap Kate in it. Kate clutched it gratefully.

"On a roof, where else? It's the *only* place to be on a night like this. You should try it sometimes."

"No, thanks." Susannah put an arm around Kate's shoulders. "Come on, let's have you checked out. Jeremy, you, too! You look almost as bad as she does. What happened to your face?"

As they walked, Will on one side of the couple, Susannah on the other, Kate and Jeremy both began talking at once. Susannah felt a knee-weakening sense of relief. Abby was okay. Sam was okay, and his friends. Now, Kate and Jeremy were finally back, and both were intact and breathing.

And they were all safe at Med Center, where they belonged.

"You were on a *roof?*" she asked happily.

At Rehab, Sid and Abby were helping pass out breakfast trays in the main room, now packed wall to wall with pallets and mattresses and cots, with people and their belongings. Volunteers moved back and forth offering food and hot drinks. It was crowded and noisy, but Abby was too busy to notice. The flood refugees looked so lost and bewildered. The hot coffee and food seemed to help.

She had spoken to her mother on the telephone and been given permission to spend the day at Med Center if necessary, now that her younger sisters were safely at home. The last thing her mother had said to her on the phone was, "I'm very proud of you, Abby. When I think of what could have happened . . ."

"Well, *don't* think of it," Abby had said. "I'm

not going to. Ever. I'll call again later when I know what time I'll be home."

"So, I hear you're a hero," Sid said as they passed out trays of scrambled eggs and toast. "People are talking."

"It was really Callie," Abby said, handing a small boy a carton of orange juice. "She's a better swimmer than I am."

He grinned. "Yeah, I heard *that*, too. From Callie, of course. To hear her tell it, you're going to owe her for the rest of your life. She's probably in the office, printing up a bill right this minute. And from what I know about Callie Matthews, you'd better pay up, or *else!*"

Abby laughed. "Yeah, I know that about her, too. Everyone does. Just the same, she did save Carmel. And I *do* owe her. Anyway, probably all she'll want is a date with some hunky football player." The instant the words left her mouth, she was aghast. How could she have said that to Sid?

Her face white, she half-turned to face him, dreading the expression of fury he would have on his face. Or of pain.

She was amazed to see that he was regarding her calmly, his dark eyes on hers. She saw no sign of anger or pain. "I'm . . . I'm sorry," she stammered. "I forgot."

He nodded. "I know." He shrugged. "That's okay with me. It'd be neat if everyone would forget the old Sid. You know, all that football-hero stuff. It'd make it easier."

Abby nodded. "I guess it would." Then she added boldly, "Callie Matthews would be lucky to date someone like you. I mean, I know you've been down here since last night. Susannah told me. You have to be really beat. But you're still here." She turned all the way around to face him fully. "There are heroes, and then there are *heroes*, right?" Holding the tray under one arm, she clapped her hands. "That round of applause is for you, Sid Costello."

"I liked the other applause better," he said boldly, turning his head to grin up at her. "I mean, I liked the reason for it better. Anyone can hand out towels. Not just anyone gets a kiss from Abby O'Connor, right?"

"This is true. I'm *very* particular about that."

He nodded soberly. "I knew that about you. Think you could spare one more? I mean, if you *really* think I'm a hero. They always get kissed in the movies,"

"This is not a movie, Sid." Abby knew everyone was watching them. She didn't care. "And you *have* been rude to me. I haven't forgotten."

"It'll never happen again."

"Sure it will. People don't change that much in one night." Abby pretended to think seriously. "But . . . these people *do* look depressed again. And I *am* a volunteer. If another kiss will cheer them up the way it did before, I should give in."

"Force yourself."

Actually, it took no effort at all on Abby's part.

This time, there was loud cheering as well as applause.

chapter
22

~~~

The worst was still ahead for the city of Grant and its residents.

First, they had to wait for the water to recede. Then they prayed for the sun to shine, to do its part in drying up the oozing mud and smelly silt. And then they began the cleanup.

The hardest-hit areas were south, east, and central Grant. Volunteers went into all of those areas, helping merchants and homeowners sift through the devastation for their belongings. People from north and west Grant, for the most part unaffected by the flood, showed up in droves to help with the cleanup. Sam and his friends were there. As well as Susannah's parents, looking very young in jeans and matching plaid shirts. The only occasions on which she'd ever seen her parents in such casual clothing were when her mother gardened and her father went fishing. They looked more . . . approachable in jeans.

There were twelve dead. Less than the last serious flood. And as Abby pointed out to Susannah while they picked through layers of mud in Eastridge, helping Kate and her family pick out and clean off cherished possessions, "Only four of those died at Med Center. The three burn patients, and the cardiac case. Pete Dawes, Curtis Brock, and the two parents trapped in the truck were already beyond hope when they arrived in ER. The others, the flood victims found in their cars or along the riverbank, never had any hope. A lot of people lived because of Emsee."

Susannah gingerly lifted a glass vase out of the mud surrounding the small yellow house. "That's true. Little Louie Murphy went home yesterday. No brain damage, thank God. Becka's going home tomorrow. The pregnant woman we were all so worried about is okay, and expects to go to full-term. Callie's fine, especially now that her picture's been in the paper, along with Sid's, in that story 'Heroes of the Flood.' I've never seen Callie so thrilled. Even her father seemed impressed. He was showing it to everyone in ER."

"Well, she does deserve it," Abby said. "If it hadn't been for Callie, Carmel could be . . . well, Carmel might not have made it. So whatever fuss is made over Callie suits me fine."

"Well," Susannah said, "Callie wasn't the only hero. There's Jeremy, saving Kate from that rooftop. And," she continued with a sly grin, "then there's that boy at Rehab. What's his name? Sid something, isn't it?"

Abby's cheeks deepened in color. "Sid Costello."

"Oh, yeah, Costello, that's right." Susannah hauled a wooden footstool up out of the debris and began wiping it with a wet rag. "You know, it's weird, but he told me you were *his* volunteer." The sly smile spread. "Imagine that? Go figure. As if you'd ever treat one patient better than another. I mean, we *were* warned about that, remember?"

Abby, her head bent, seemed to be concentrating intently on wiping completely clean two pieces of silverware she'd unearthed. "Yeah, we were," she muttered. "Wouldn't want to break any rules, would we? Not even if someone needed us to. I mean, *really* needed us to."

Susannah laughed. "I heard about the kiss, Abby. Everyone did. And he *is* cute. His manners are rotten, though."

Abby lifted her head. She looked relieved, and was grinning. "Yeah, well, I'm working on that."

At least a dozen times that day, someone said, in the midst of all the filth and muck and debris, "It could have been much worse."

Susannah knew they were right. It could have. If it hadn't been for Emsee, there would have been a lot more deaths.

It was Sam's idea, of course, to throw a Flood Cleanup Party at Rehab. When he suggested it that night in front of Will's house, to a group of filthy, exhausted volunteers, Susannah laughed. "Another party? Oh, honestly, Sam, you just never stop, do you?"

But she loved the idea.

And she had a wonderful time. Half the city came. Callie Matthews spent the entire evening telling all who would listen the graphic details of her harrowing rescue of a small child in floodwaters, embroidering the story further each time she told it. There were other, truer stories of rescues, but Callie's voice was the loudest and the most insistent, not to mention the rudest whenever someone became bored and turned away from her.

Ignoring Callie's shrill voice wasn't easy, but Abby managed, dancing the night away with Sid. She sat on his lap, her arms around his neck, as he spun the wheelchair around. They laughed a lot.

Susannah and Will danced past Kate and Jeremy, sitting at a table arguing about her refusal to take swim lessons at the Y. "But I don't want to!" she was saying, and Jeremy, to Susannah's surprise, responded matter-of-factly, "Well, I can't be there to save you every time there's a flood."

Becka hadn't recovered enough to attend the party.

"I'm not sure she would have, anyway," Sam told Susannah. "Couldn't blame her if she stayed home. Maybe she hates me."

"Not in a million years," Susannah said. "She's nuts about you, like practically every other female in this city." She glanced around the room, telling herself silently that she'd been one of the lucky ones. She hadn't lost someone close to her to the floodwaters. There was Will, in a corner talking to Abby and Sid and Jeremy, and Kate was dancing by in the arms of some tall, lanky boy Susannah didn't know. Her parents had just arrived, her mother in blue silk. And her twin brother was standing right beside her. There were people in Grant who hadn't been as lucky. "Anyway," Susannah added, watching as Will left the others and began walking toward her, "you could always remind Becka that you saved her life."

"And she could remind me that I was the reason she *needed* saving in the first place," Sam said. "Wouldn't blame her." Then a small, pretty blonde girl came along and claimed him.

Will returned to Susannah's side a moment later. He looked very handsome in khaki pants and a red turtleneck sweater.

"About that clinic," Susannah said, smiling up at him. "I have some questions."

"How about," he said, taking her hand, "I answer them while we dance? I think better to music."

He took her in his arms and rested his cheek on the top of her head.

That suited Susannah just fine.

An exciting excerpt from *Fire*, Med Center #3, coming next.

———∿∿∿∿∿∿∿———

On the grounds of Grant Petroleum Products, a sprawling complex of oil tanks, office buildings, and warehouses, the darkness and quiet of a basement closet was broken by a sudden sharp, spitting sound, followed by a duller hissing noise. Then a shower of golden, fiery sparks, like a cluster of fireflies, shot out of a large black electrical box fastened on one wall.

When the sparks and the hissing had died, there was silence again in the dim enclosure.

But minutes later, a tiny puff of smoke curled out from under the edges of the big black box on the wall. The box serviced one of several office buildings on the site, which spread across thickly wooded acreage in the city of Grant, Massachusetts. The office building, tall and wide and constructed entirely of red brick, had been built close to one of the huge, round oil tanks.

"Shouldn't be puttin' a building this close to

the tanks," one of the construction workers had been heard to mutter while working on the site years earlier. "If old Titus Grant wasn't so tight with money, they'd be spreadin' this place out a little more, keepin' all the buildings away from the tanks. Me, I been around refineries all my life. Ain't seen one yet that didn't have a fire at least once a year. This one won't be no different. Shouldn't be puttin' no buildings this close."

But no one paid the slightest bit of attention to his objections. Although the refinery complex had grown over the years, the office building had stayed where it was, side-by-side with the cluster of oil tanks.

Now, the tiny puff of smoke grew. At first, it stayed close to the black box, trailing around its outside edges like a curling, gray vine. Then, fueled by oxygen in the air, it blossomed. Eager to explore its surroundings, it left the black box and began lazily easing its way up the basement wall toward the ceiling. As it did so, a small, bright, orange-red flame stabbed its way out of the box, looked to see where the puff of smoke had gone, and decided to follow it.

The smoke and its tagalong partner, the flame, seemed to be in no particular hurry. They took their time easing along the wall, like children exploring new territory.

But as they went, they grew in size.

Miles away, in the center of the city, in another sprawling complex of taller, newer brick buildings known as Med Center, the staff settled in for a Saturday of meeting every kind of medical emergency and rendering every kind of medical care. They were blissfully unaware of the refinery's lazy, trailing smoke and its companion, the flame. So they had no way of knowing what horrors were in store for them on this unusually balmy, windy Saturday in late October.

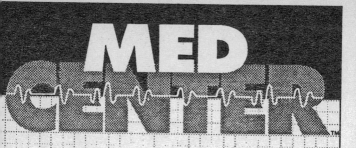

MED CENTER

The action at Med Center is getting even hotter....

A raging fire sweeps through Grant, taking over the lives of everyone in the city. Amid the nonstop turmoil, the Med Center workers struggle to deal with a growing number of victims...and the fire that's getting closer and closer.

fire

MED CENTER #3

BY DIANE HOH

Coming soon to a bookstore near you.